Th

Tree

Whisperers

MARY FREDA
WILSON

PIPIT

For Ruth, Max and Lawrence

'It is possible to live in the twilight between knowing and not knowing.'

H A Visser't Hooft

Prologue

Southern Italy – July 1998

THE glare of the summer's day bounces off the limestone rock. Leon carefully negotiates the hairpin bends, occasionally glancing at Kay. In spite of the giddying ravines dropping down from her side of the car, she seems relaxed. Up to a point, he feels energised to be bringing her here to this place after all this time; even though it involves a funeral.

It's just that she's asking about his past again. Or as some people call it: the incident, or that awful thing that happened. He suspects she senses some things remain unaccounted for. And now, out here, she's dipping into what lies beyond the unsaid, putting him on edge.

"I'm glad you came with me," he says.

But he's not that sure. For as well as the gentle probing, her presence could put a brake on the things he'd like to say to people, making it hard to step where he needs to tread.

"Me too!" Her hair streams in the wind as she smiles across at him.

Like many women he's known, Kay is emotionally alert, sensing and picking up on things.

She recently asked, after one of their bolder sexual encounters:

"So, do you still love her then, just a teeny bit?"

"Love Sue, you mean?"

"Yes, Sue. Your ex-wife."

"No, I do not."

And yet he half knows she remains between them still. Gone from his life, but troubling.

As they exit another bend, Kay points out a V of Canadian

geese. 'Where are they going? Somewhere to feed, or to breed?"

"Both, probably."

Strange, he thinks, how sexual intimacy can co-exist with emotional restraint. But with further thought, he imagines it might be quite usual.

Southern Italy – May 1987

LEON opened his eyes, and winced. His head was pommeling and his throat was dry – he'd emptied the mini bar. He hauled himself up in bed before edging his feet out and onto the floor, then crossing his room to the balcony. Moonlight scattered the water. It looked like some ghostly walkway, reminding him of the Yellow Brick Road and his daughter's love of that Julie Garland movie. Thoughts of Maria twitched and twirled, that old persistent pain scratching away again, so he switched his gaze to the land where he picked out Vesuvius, brooding silently. Such was his life, he thought – an extinct volcano. What was the point of trying to make any good of it?

It was when he climbed back into bed that he heard the noise. Was that what had roused him, and not the moon? It sounded like snoring. Maybe a guest in an adjacent room. But no, too gentle for that, it was more like sighing. The breeze then perhaps, gently winnowing through the trees.

The following morning, Leon waited impatiently in the dining room for his breakfast coffee. He'd never been good in the early morning, and today he was fragile. His temples throbbed as he ate some fruit and cereal, the head waiter bobbing amongst the guests, making dramatic flourishes.

He began to speculate about this man. Didn't his job involve playing a part, like his own had? Both men were seasoned masters of feigning empathy and bonhomie. Both hid behind a uniform. The waiter had his penguin suit, while Leon had his wig, his piercings, his thickly framed glasses, his stage make-up...

Both jobs provided an escape. The waiter's, into a world of flamboyant gestures, joviality, even tricks. A napkin unfurled with a flick of the wrist; a surprise desert magicked out of the kitchen. His own: into a world of telepathy, magic, hypnotism and the power to suspend disbelief. It was all the antithesis of what Leon truly believed in – logic, empiricism, atheism, skepticism, an absence of natural justice in the world.

He studied the waiter again, wondering where things diverged. He had to be much more worldly than the waiter, surely? Furthermore, he was rich. Very – for someone aged only forty-three. He smiled to himself, thinking how he could buy this hotel outright. But he wouldn't be travelling the globe in the future. And he wouldn't be stepping onstage again.

His coffee arrived. He gulped his first cup down, then made his way to the breakfast counter to fill his plate with pecorino cheese and cold ham. On his way back, he noticed a tree. A tree? In a restaurant? He stood there with his plate, staring. It was enclosed by a fence, its gnarled and mottled trunk – massive in girth – rising up through the woven roof of the extended dining area. The upper half of its trunk was bound in thick plastic, he assumed to prevent any bugs from falling into people's risottos.

Back at his table, he thought how a tree in a dining room was just as bizarre as a central hotel area open to the elements. It annoyed him having to walk through that hot and sticky place, jumping with insects, crowded with overgrown fronds, bristling with prickly shrubs that seemed to reach out for you. But it was the quickest route to his bedroom.

The sun was spilling through the open doorway of the hotel, enticing Leon from the foyer and into the grounds. It was only mid-morning, so he had the rest of the day before Greta, his agent, arrived tomorrow. She worked in an agency specialising in designer breaks for the very well-heeled. His own interest was in genealogy, and she'd already begun some research on his behalf. And why shouldn't he pay through the nose for someone to do the all work? In any case, he needed a translator – for as his Italian grandmother scathingly reminded him – he spoke not a word of the language. This quest was his promise to her. His promise to himself was to replace the dross in his head with something meaningful, then hopefully he could move on. Kay wanted that.

He walked across the parking area and towards the viewing terrace, with its sea views of the bay. He liked that the hotel was secluded, situated high up the cliff, close to the mountains. It was at the end of a long dirt drive, forking off the narrow road that zigzagged its way to the half-deserted village where his family came from.

Below him he could see the town, with its tightly packed streets, dots of trees and bursts of bougainvillea. He could just about make out the deep ravine carved out two centuries ago by an earthquake. Wondering why most of the hotel grounds had been given over to olive groves, he set off to walk down the steep cliff path and explore, in search of late morning beers and a double espresso, pocketing a handful of pine cones along the way.

But with each turn of the track, he looked back – an impulse hard to break, following years of being followed.

The next day was humid and overcast. The heat was too much for him; his damp shirt already clinging to the skin on his back. Yesterday's mosquito bites, scattered around his ankles, were oozing puss and lowering his mood. But he'd remembered to bring the picture, now safe and snug in a hessian hold-all on the back seat of his guide's car. Greta was cheerily chatty as they drove along, more familiar with him than he'd expect for a first meeting. Thick curls tumbled around her neck, a grin bordering on cheeky. She explained how she was bilingual, her mother of farming stock from outside Dublin, her father reared near here. The road to 'his' village was poorly maintained, but Greta was practiced at skirting the potholes.

"I've learnt quite a lot about your family roots here," she said. "I'll tell you about it as we look around."

"Fine. I forgot to tell you about my grandmother's great uncle Bengie. An eccentric type, living in the woods as a recluse before he joined a local religious order."

"It was the easiest way to make yourself scarce in those heavily-wooded days," she said. "I'll check him out for you. But the name must be spelled the Italian way, as in B-e-n-g-h-i?"

"You would know, I'm sure."

She nods. "His surname?"

"Catelli."

"Okay. So, your family is religious, yes?"

"I'm an atheist." He found her directness irritating.

"Ah. But you can't prove there's no God, can you? So, wouldn't you prefer the word 'agnostic'?"

He shrugged. "Are you a believer, then?"

"Well, I do not believe in a god . . . but I do believe in something." She hesitated. "I have faith in people, in their capacity to transcend things. I believe in kindness, and in how all things are interconnected."

He sighed, imagining things like witchcraft, nature-worshipping, veganism . . . He supposed she was rather like his daughter Maria, someone never without a cause. Global warming, animal rights, multiculturalism. He'd known how to press her buttons – like pretending he was a climate change denier. He would talk to her differently now, he would show her more respect. That scratchy, tightening feeling was clutching away again; always worse when rummaging through things left unsaid, not done, never to be put right.

"There's safety in your agnostic belief system Leon – it's not going to cause wars."

"Very true."

They were pulling up in the village square. It felt unreal to at last be glimpsing this sleepy, run-down place of his family's past. Part of him feared learning new things about his past, in case they threw up something unpalatable. He was supposed to have come here with Maria – he'd promised her. He sighed, pulling his thoughts away, snapping his fingers in Greta's face while discretely slipping the other hand into his pocket. She gasped as yesterday's pine cones sprouted, then vanished from his fingers. For him, the routine was basic, but she threw back her head and emitted a series of wows.

8

He grinned. "It's my occupation. Correction, it used to be..."

"You gave it up? How could you, when you're so good?"

He told her he neither needed nor wanted to work anymore, that a family accident had put an end to it. Pleased she hadn't guessed his identity, and keen to stifle any further questioning, he reached into the rear seat for his hold-all, retrieving the picture and peeling back the wrapping.

Greta peered across at it. "My goodness Leon, this is amazing."

The photograph had haunted Leon throughout his childhood. So many unsmiling faces and staring eyes, as if penetrating his soul. His mother had framed it just after his father had died. Leon had been just thirteen; and had gone on to associate it with that turbulent time. It captured a large group of horticultural workers, arranged in majestic rows. The men were slim and strong-muscled, smartly waist-coated, bristling with watch chains and braces. Like a weapon of combat, each held a scythe or other tool of the kind you might find in a museum. The boy Leon, lying awake at night, would fear that if he slept one of the men would climb from the frame and attack him.

Greta grinned in excitement: "It looks mid eighteen-hundreds – you should check on the back for an inscription. They're clearly Italian, you can tell from the tools. Most would be family, the better dressed ones I suspect." She paused. "Your family was working the land much earlier though, cultivating a strip higher up the hillside. I'd like to take you there and show you."

9

Leon decided his guide was earning her money well. He was impressed by her, even nervous of her, but not sexually attracted. Already, he was missing Kay more than he'd expected. At first, he'd been scared of not pleasing her sexually, but she'd brought some fun into it – so that alongside the hunger and passion it had felt like play.

Strolling around the village, he found Greta's knowledge to be rich and detailed. She pointed out the dwellings and places of significance – who, when, and how they would have lived there. Her account was so vivid that Leon could visualise living amongst them. The ambience of those times seemed to swirl around and cling to him – the demands of hard physical labour, the smell of dung and sweat, the sounds of hooves on the cobbles and women's chatter as they rinsed their linen in the stream. A sense of connection stirred, surprising and discomfiting him.

The path up the hillside was steep, but dry and firm. The air was sharp and clean; his lungs seemed to welcome it. Every so often he stopped, turned back and scanned how far they'd scrambled. A thin bank of sea fret sat on the horizon. There was a sweet scent of pines, and he noticed a tree like the one in the dining area. He pointed this out, and Greta told him its local name was umbrella tree. She brought things to his attention he wouldn't have noticed: a ridge of the granite used to build his hotel, the gleam of the sun on the skin of a scurrying lizard. She identified the calls of sea birds, pointed out a swallowtail butterfly napping on a secluded leaf, and a half-camouflaged mountain goat. As she chatted, he noticed the muted sounds of the sea and the sharp blue stars of convolvulus blooms poking through the growth. The more they climbed, the more he felt the tightness inside him slackening off.

The remains of an ancient watchtower came into view. Not far beyond that, on a small outgrowth, stood some jagged and hostile-looking boulders, precariously poised as if ready to fling themselves into their path. He stared back as they continued climbing, thinking he saw something lurking there.

"Over here," Greta beckoned, pointing towards a track leading off to a hollowed-out part of the hillside, opening into a long, flat and sheltered area. "It's your family's land strip!"

He walked across to her, scanning the barren scrub, finding little evidence of past activity apart from a tumbled down shed which Greta said would have held livestock and tools. She explained how the strip would have been a great 'find', fertile soil being scarce amongst these rocky hills, and how it became the embryo of the family's burgeoning market-gardening business.

The strip was well protected from the wind, but as she continued to feed more details, he started to wilt in the mid-day sun. The heat was further aggravating his mosquito bites, and he thanked his luck at escaping the family's heritage of working on the land. The charm of pastoral novels and landscape paintings had always escaped him, as had gambolling lambs, poetic sunrises and birdsong. As a child he'd dreaded family car runs to the countryside, the smell of petrol and his father's pipe, always inducing car sickness. Wordsworth had bored him, and he hated learning poems by rote. The natural world with its 'wonders' – the feel in your hand of the honest goodness in the soil, the wonder of crocus and daffodil pushing up through it – was thrust at him by his parents and by his grandmother.

As then, as now – it meant nothing to him. But something about being up in these hills was comforting, as if he'd always known them. And Greta was companionable.

"I've just realised," said Greta, straightening up in her seat as a waiter served them beers and a light salad back at their hotel. "This religious ancestor of yours – he could be linked to the Abbey."

"Abbey?"

"This one."

"How do you mean?"

"Oh . . . you don't know this hotel used to be an abbey?"

Leon shook his head.

"Some kind of unorthodox religious retreat. You didn't notice the open cloister in the centre of the building? And the olive groves? – they provided the village with olive oil – that's how the monks supported themselves. Oh – and the head waiter, Raphael, he knows a few things about them. If you're interested, you could talk to him."

But Leon wasn't sure he wanted to talk to the man, he'd rather Greta collected the information herself. It was Gran he was doing this for and the bare bones of things would suffice. The past played little part in his present, and certainly not in his future.

After agreeing a time to visit the nearest town, Leon said goodbye and went to his room to apply some cream to his bites. Within minutes he was asleep on his bed. On waking, he mused about having dreamed he was Benghi, dressed in monastic habit, tending olives. He showered, then drifted through to the bar, ordering the first of three glasses of the local wine, then failed to enjoy his evening meal, having lost his appetite. Pushing aside his plate of baked aubergine, he left the restaurant, pausing to whisper a sardonic *dormi bene* to the tree. He tried to settle on his balcony with a scotch from the minibar, but the wrought iron bench was uncomfortable, and Vesuvius was clothed in heavy mist.

Back in his room, undressing and coiling more cream round his ankles, he heard the wistful noise again. Somewhere between sobbing and singing, making him think of choral chants. Pacing around, he noticed the grid from the air-com system, deciding that must be the source of the sound. By the time he climbed into bed and was close to sleep, it had changed and become more comforting. Like the sound of a stretched-out cat, purring into the night.

|2|

Greta was taking the weekend off. Welcoming this chance of some space and partly adjusted to the heat, he spent time in the hotel grounds, exploring the orchards, the kitchen gardens, and the pathways down the cliff side. From time to time he retreated to an armchair on the terrace off the dining room, to read Stephen King's *The Shining*, a book he'd spotted on a bookshelf outside his room.

During one of his garden strolls, he came across what looked a lily pond, ornamental in design, with a fountain at its centre. But it was empty, drained of water deliberately, he thought. Its inky depths glowered back at him as if offering up some toxic secret. His ex-wife Sue had ruled against such ponds as a danger to inquisitive children.

His mind strayed into the fault lines of their past relationship: how she hadn't welcomed his acquired wealth, and what she called his unhealthy retreat into his on-stage character. She'd preferred his amateur conjuring days of kiddies' birthday parties. Maybe he had too? The parents had been as much in awe as their kids, and he'd always had a few jokes for them, weaving double entendres into his act.

While at the pond he had a sense of being watched, and thought he glimpsed some twitching near a stone shed, some distance away. He waited for a while before strolling over. It was a nondescript building, perhaps a shelter for people working in the olive groves. The area behind it was clear.

Returning to his room, his phone was ringing. It was Frank, his agent.

"Leon – I have a guy here who's been nagging about a commission for you to entertain some Royals on their yacht. The Caribbean. Why not considerate it?"

"No, Frank. As I told you, it's a 'no' to everything. I'm mothballed, remember? Be a good gatekeeper, Frank. Please."

Back in the dining room, drinking more beers before his lunch, he noticed the fenced off tree wasn't looking that healthy. Compared with the ones he'd spotted up the hillside it seemed rather sad and droopy, perhaps short of water. Fed up, he decided, without any choice but to listen to the drivel of half-pissed diners.

Most days he ventured down the hillside for a swim at the old fishing port, followed by a light lunch (he was body-swerving the hotel pool, to avoid contact with other residents). There he enjoyed his fill of the finest foods, oysters and lobsters especially, the best available bottle of Franciacorta, and the eventual words of the waiter – *muchas gracias Signore* – graciously delivered on receipt of his generous tip.

Arriving at the village one Sunday, having broken his walk to stop for his beers, Leon sat down on a bench and looked around him, trying to imagine the port as unspoiled, stripped of modern-day tourism. Surprised at his own sentimentality, he went on to imagine its blemishes . . . the stench of rotting fish, untidy nets stretched out in the sun, knots of dirty children, and other signs of poverty. He stood up to walk over to a stall of snorkelling equipment, and hired some.

Trailing along the water's surface, he returned to a world of childhood holidays. His father unpersuaded to join him in the water, while his mother would have put herself on show, preening, sighing, mulling over her ailments. He'd had no siblings to distract him. He edged his way along the water's surface, enjoying the feel of the sliding water as he searched for crabs and whelks, as his boyhood self would have done, a sense of freedom spilling through him, the water's swell and the shoals of tiny fish winking and wrinkling around him.

For locals, Sunday was the day for families. His late and peaceful lunch was interrupted by an Italian couple and their daughter, politely asking to share his table. The girl was Maria's age, she had that same sulky sensuality. The family's closeness, shown in their smiles, touches and gestures, sheared open his loss.

Polite enquiries were exchanged: "Are you staying here long?" "Do you live nearby?" Leon asked if they knew the history of the village. No, they did not. Their daughter fiddled with her hair, staring out to sea with no attempt to conceal her boredom. Just like Maria.

His ache had only slightly eased as he climbed his way back up the hill, pausing half way to turn and glance at the view of the coastline, imagining taking this in with Maria. He thought how he'd failed to bring her here, how they'd argued about it. When she was eleven years old they'd written a song, they'd done it for Gran. He began to sing it, but soon was faltering. The next minute he was weeping, smudging the tears away, embarrassed, though no one was watching. He impatiently crushed his thoughts, as if with his shoe he was crushing the lizard that Greta had pointed out to him.

As he was dressing for dinner, a call came in from his housekeeper. She was confirming dates for his building foundations survey, to establish the feasibility of a basement cinema. Out here, his notion seemed quite fanciful, even fatuous. Had it sprung from boredom? Might he be losing the plot on how to spend his money? These days he received few personal calls, and he and Kay had agreed not to be in touch. She wanted some space to test their relationship, especially his handling of alcohol. Were people giving up on him? Was he becoming a grumpy recluse? Perhaps that was Benghi's problem. Why he lived in the woods, why he had joined that retreat.

Walking into the dining room, he noticed some sap glistening on the tree's trunk. Surreptitiously, he traced a finger through it, then put it to his lips. It tasted salty, just like tears.

Greta phoned the following morning to say she was going to be late. It was due, she said, to a deterioration in the health of a neighbour's boy she'd been helping to look after. Leon settled himself outside on the dining room verandah, happy to pass the time by resuming reading *The Shining*. He'd been slightly unsettled to find it was set in a hotel – albeit an American one – but which like his own nestled in the mountains.

Greta arrived with apologies, and as they drove into town, began to talk about the boy, Pietro, just turned aged thirteen. Leon listened, more interested in the passing scenery than what she had to say, until she mentioned that the boy's father was Raphael, his head waiter.

"Pietro used to come up to the hotel after school and in the school holidays. He earned pocket money by helping out, especially in the olive grove. He developed an interest in all of the trees, researched them and cared for them, even drew sketches of them, all collected in a book which he called his tree family album. Olives of course, but also the stone pine, cherry laurel, evergreen oak. For Pietro, it became an obsession. The hotel manager gave him a new name: the tree whisperer."

"Tree whisperer?" Leon pondered this. "What about that tree in the dining room, then? The one wrapped up in plastic. Did he tend to that one as well?"

"That old umbrella tree? Of course. It was his favourite. He hated that they built the dining room extension around it. He said the tree was hating it, too."

Leon smiled. He was about to say he too thought the tree was unhappy, but enquired instead about Pietro's health condition. But Greta was reluctant to expand, apart from saying that something tragic had happened.

"Leon – if you plan to talk to Raphael about the hotel's history, please don't mention Pietro. Raphael wouldn't like to think we've been talking about his boy."

On the outskirts of the town, they stopped to pick up a horticultural historian, a scruffy looking man Leon thought, but knowledgeable and friendly. They first called at an area cultivating figs and tomatoes, gobbo (a kind of artichoke) and oranges – the latter cheap enough to be eaten abundantly by the very poor. Their guide pointed out the wooden props traditionally used to protect and train the growth, how reeds were used to build the trellises, and the way the wells were harnessed to augment irrigation. He pulled out some photos from his briefcase, identifying one of an aerial view of the site.

"Look, Signore Leon," he said, pointing to a section of the photo. "Here are these plots we've been looking at. For some years they were your people's land, after they left behind that land strip that Greta showed you." He then pointed to another, more expansive area. "And this is where we are going to next."

They drove on into a district on the east side of the city, still profiting, they were told, from the cultivated sandy peninsular soil which in earlier times was submerged by the sea. The guide pointed out the boundaries of what used to be his family's business, eventually sold off between the two world wars. The land was now intensively worked for productive yields of tomato and other soft fruit, the crops thriving within looping plastic Nissen-hut-style enclosures. The black ugliness of these structures seemed to complement the surrounding blighted urban settlements and interlocking sections of the freeway. The guide went on to speak about twentieth century innovations and the impact of mechanisation, shifting profit margins, genetic advances, market competition and branding strategies. For Leon, this was a turn-off; he was relieved to see the man checking his watch and apologising for having to rush for his train.

Leon suggested a local but quiet bar where they could reflect on their trip's findings. But, once settled with their drinks at a shady outside table, Greta changed the conversation by gently probing about his 'accident'. He skilfully steered the focus away, enquiring of her family and her childhood, and then her working life.

"Am I happy with my job? Well, being a guide isn't fully where I want to be, but I try and give it my best. It keeps me in food and rent, while I put my true energies into developing my practice."

"Your practice?"

"I volunteer at a local centre for people needing psychological help. My special interest is trauma. I don't get paid, but I get good training, and once my skills have been accredited, I plan to set up my own practice. My dream is to develop my own centre; some friends have said they will help me raise the money. This is my hope, to take my real work further, build skills and knowledge around alternative therapies, give the field a new direction."

He looked away for a moment, thinking of Maria and her zany ideas about meditation and past life regression. He believed that people should be responsible for themselves, build resilience, refrain from self-pity – like he'd had to do when Maria died.

Greta caught and held his gaze. "It doesn't grab you, does it? You are so easy to read, Leon . . ."

"No, it all sounds very worthy. Charity, therapy, counselling, I'm sure there is a place for it." He said this in spite of his experience that nothing had helped him. Especially the bereavement support group the hospital had bullied him into attending, a few days after pumping his stomach. Alcohol and sleeping pills. It wasn't that he'd given up on life, he'd just been careless. Two days before that he'd been drunk and escorted off stage. But at the group, he'd met Kay. He hadn't fancied her at first, but was struck by her candour and insight. Scared of it, too.

"But I can be a little skeptical," he continued, beckoning the waiter for another beer. "You can't stop cancer in its tracks, by offering these fringe alternatives, can you? I mean, where is the evidence base?"

Greta smiled, shaking her head.

He smiled back. "So, who would benefit from your dream retreat?"

"You want examples? Okay. There's Pietro, Raphael's son, for a start." She explained how he'd witnessed a tragic accident, was traumatised, blaming himself, unable to return to school. A child he'd sometimes helped to look after was playing by the hotel lily pond. When Pietro heard the commotion, it was too late, the child had drowned. He pulled him out, frantically tried to revive him. But it was all too late.

Leon shuddered. "I noticed that pond. But where were the parents?"

"They were there. But the father had been stung by a bee, he was allergic to stings, and his wife was busy helping him."

"Pietro should not have blamed himself."

"But it happens. So now do you see the need for my centre?"

He nodded. And to his surprise, some of his own past slipped out. About his own 'accident', involving his wife witnessing the death of their daughter. About how he sympathised with this Pietro, as he too knew how guilt anchors deep inside you. But on hearing his own words he began to regret them, reining himself in when she enquired some more, changing the subject.

Greta dropped him back at the hotel, explaining she would contact him about a visit to the Cathedral archives, to seek out further information about Benghi. She also made him promise not to mention Pietro to Raphael. He shut the car door, feeling unsettled.

Taking the shortcut towards his room, something seemed to stir amongst the spikes of the aloe vera plants, and ripple through the bougainvillea. He shrugged, thinking it must be the effects of reading *The Shining*, with its hotel's bourgeoning menace encroaching on the protagonist's life.

At first, Leon had no intention of talking to Raphael. But he frequently found himself thinking about the man's son, imagining what life was like for a boy trapped in guilt over a drowning. He felt sympathy for the boy, and from this flowed a curiosity about the father.

Mid-week, he hung back after breakfast, waiting for the other guests to leave so he could approach him. The man seemed surprised, perhaps having judged Leon as an isolate, but eagerly fell into a detailed and meandering tale about the hotel's history, all the way back to its site being that of a pagan temple. He described his time growing up in the village where Leon's family came from, and how a distant relative of his own had entered the monastic retreat.

"Was it a cult of some kind?" Leon asked. "Or a genuine place of faith?"

Raphael frowned, as if unsure how to answer. "They claimed they were monks, and named themselves the Order. The community outside, it was in two halves of beliefs. But whether it was a good or a bad place, it was a best thing for the olive trees. They say the trees had whisperers. You know – tree whisperers."

"Tree whisperers?"

"People for to cherish the trees. To tend of them, speak with them, caress of them. The legend was that persons who ate the olive oil, the person lived longer, they lived a life that was more caring, more fruitful. Thus, it is how, these cherished trees, that they rewarded the people who cared for them."

Leon thought back to what Greta had told him, hoping the waiter would mention Pietro. "Does anyone whisper to them now? Now the hotel is no longer a retreat?"

"Indeed, there is. It is the job of my dear son, Pietro. He became the keeper, the whisperer. He loved, he knew each tree here, from just as he was a young boy. He said they spoke, that they leaned in to him. He knew when they were having the thirst, when they had a threat like a nasty disease, or a drought. He said he could hear of their pain, and their hurt.' He gave an exasperated sigh. 'I don't know why I tell it to you – you think it crazy, yes? In any case, my son is not now coming amongst his trees. He is unwell. But that is my private matter."

"I'm sorry to hear that, Raphael. And please – I do respect your privacy – I will not intrude." He told him instead about Benghi, that he and Greta were visiting the cathedral tomorrow in search of more information about him.

"Aha! You both go to the cathedral? In which case, I have something that please you might take there. We found it in a trunk in the garden cellars, they lie underneath in the old shed that was once for the gardeners. Some papers there, all in books of leather, I think the word to use for this is 'logs'? The manager says they must go to the Cathedral, to be there for the archives; they are from the time of the Order."

"Of course, we'll take them."

"Thank you. I will tell that someone must leave them in your room."

| 3 |

Once Greta arrived, Leon led her to two seats in the shade of the garden, carrying the box with the leather-bound logs. She eagerly took these from him, offering to translate. The entries were made in the style of ledgers, in exquisitely formed handwriting, and Greta went on to explain they were a record of the trees, each one numbered and classified weekly as to their state of health and any action taken to revive, nourish or otherwise care for them. Some had been named. At the front of the ledger there was a meticulously drawn garden map, fully to scale, with each tree carefully identified.

"It's kept up to date until 1864. I wonder how long the Order was here for?"

"I'm not sure. In the late Middle Ages the building was a catholic monastery, closed down in the second half of the 17th century. In those days the monarchist elite disenfranchised most of the conventional catholic monasteries in southern Italy. But of course, the catholic church in its turn would have confiscated the land from the original pagans who had worshipped on the same site."

He laughed. "And, so it goes on . . . now downgraded to a secular site, but still occupied by worshippers."

"How come?"

"Sun worshippers."

She laughed. "For the first time, Leon, I hear you tell a joke.

My country must be doing something for you, yes?"

He grinned.

Now she was studying a particular page. "Leon – check this!" She pointed to the initials at the foot of several entries, pushing him in the shoulder and laughing. "This looks like our Benghi! I think we've found him." She turned to the index, finding a list of residents responsible for tending the garden, and ran a finger down it. "Here he is! Chief tree guardian! This is so exciting . . ." Then she became serious. "You know, Leon – Pietro would love to see these logs, I don't know why Raphael never thought of it."

"I'm sure Pietro would. Could we show them to him? I mean, show him now, before we take them to the cathedral? Is there enough time?"

Pietro's home was on the town's outskirts, at the point where the land begins to rise into the hills. They parked and set off walking, Leon carrying a bag of books he'd brought to lend him, chosen from the shelf outside his room. There was a refreshing breeze, and Leon picked up the scent of the flowers bobbing away on the other side of people's walls. He was feeling invigorated by the exercise and the thought of meeting Pietro. Greta pointed out her own home to him as they walked alongside it – the upper half of a cottage, her cat stretched out on the window sill in the early morning sun.

Then . . . wham. Back with that other cat, the dead one on his doorstep – Maria's cat.

Greta stopped, grasping his shoulder. "What's the matter, Leon?"

25

"Nothing. Nothing . . . I just remembered something . . ."

"But you look scared . . ."

"I'm fine, honestly."

They set off again, and she explained how she usually called in on the boy on her way home from work, his Gran spending late afternoon putting in a few hours at a local bakery, his mother having died from cancer four years ago. Some washing was flapping in a small plot at the side of Pietro's cottage as they arrived there, a few chickens squawking and scratching around beneath it.

Greta knocked and pushed on the door, which opened straight into the living room. The boy was sitting by the window, reading a book; he glanced across and blinked shyly at them. Leon thought he looked lanky and skinny, with a pallor to his skin; far younger than his thirteen years. His hair was thick and unkempt, with no sheen to it.

Greta spoke in Italian, introducing him to Leon, who walked over and proffered a handshake, offering his bag of books. At Greta's instigation, Pietro reluctantly replied in English, politely thanking Leon, and absentmindedly reading through the books, until his interest was caught by the one Leon had thought was a mistake to bring – a guide to the Milan Museum of Modern and Contemporary Arts. As Greta busied herself at the stove Leon pulled up a chair, and managed to strike up a halting conversation with the boy. He discovered some of his likes and dislikes, how he spent time with his friends, and who his favourite teachers were. Leon mentioned he was staying at the hotel where Pietro's father worked.

"Oh. So are the trees well?" the boy asked gloomily.

"Your trees seem happy, yes. Greta told me how you care for them. So you must miss them?"

He nodded. "The Umbrella tree – I miss her most. I named her Luna."

Greta came through with a tray, a plate piled high with scrambled eggs. "Isn't his English good? His home schooler has been giving him extra help with it." As Pietro took the plate from her, she placed a hand on his back. "We have a surprise for you, my dear. This man here knows of a tree whisperer, someone from his family, he worked with those trees long before you, those very same trees in the hotel." She pointed to the logs laid on the table. "And he wrote all about them in there."

Pietro turned to Leon: "There is a tree whisperer – in your family?"

"Yes. He's called Benghi, but he lived a long time ago."

Pietro gave Leon a quizzical look, and grinned. Then something in the boy seemed to come alive.

Once Pietro had finished eating, Greta beckoned him over, and they sat round the sturdy oak table, huddled over the logs. Speaking in both Italian and English she turned over the pages, pointing to different things, explaining the format for entering the data, providing any historical background she thought might be of interest. Throughout, she encouraged Pietro to engage and ask his own questions.

But Pietro was engrossed from the start, intrigued to discover that each member of the retreat had responsibility for a specific tree, and each tree had been named. Greta explained that while the Order insisted the high quality of their oil was due to their intimate care of the olive grove, historians later attributed it to the fertiliser, procured from fish waste from the Port. When Greta pointed out that the logs showed it was Benghi himself who planted Luna, Pietro rocked in his chair with excitement.

"The Logs," asked Pietro. "Do they tell us what the man Benghi was like?"

Greta smiled. "Well, they show us how meticulous he was."

Pietro frowned. "Meticulous? *Cosa significa*?"

"Oh, sorry. It means that he was careful, even with tiny details. He liked order, everything done well, as well as possible. And the logs show how much he loved the trees. You can tell from the way he describes each of them. There is so much careful detail, you'd think each and every one had a personality of its own."

"But every tree does!' he insisted. 'And my tree, La Luna. What does he say about La Luna?"

Greta carefully turned more pages. "Ah, here we are," she pointed. "It says here, six weeks after he's planted it, that: Tigre is fighting strong. Its branches vigorous, its trunk vital with health and energy."

"He called my tree Tigre? Not Luna?"

Greta nodded.

Pietro pondered this. "I know she likes moonlight; she best likes it when we talk in moonlight. But I can call her Luna Tigre."

Leon watched and listened, taking note of Greta, the way she fed Pietro words to fuel his interest, the way she caught his glance and smiled, the way she steered the conversation so that he felt involved. He found in her a generous attitude, a way to affirm someone's value, tease out their individuality. And as she translated the lengthier comments Pietro made in Italian, he realised how knowledgeable the boy was. Not just about the needs of trees, but those horticultural principles and practices that applied to them – knowing even that they stretched back thousands of years, originating in ancient Persia.

But Pietro had his own code of conduct with the trees. He believed in touch, in talking and even singing to them. He insisted they could feel, sense and reflect. That they have what is known as 'complex bio-sensitive spheres' – how to tolerate adverse conditions, adapt to them and eventually prosper.

"They have more patience than us, we human beings, because they live so very longer. I wish to insist, Leon, that our human communications are basic. That is in comparison with our trees. And I have learned how to sense them asking to speak with me, I can hear it in the sap as it is rising, I can pick up the whispering in their bark and from their branches."

Leon found the boy astonishing: extraordinarily knowledgeable, analytical, and articulate – even in a foreign language. A phrase Leon's father often used came back to him – 'too clever by half.' But the boy wasn't arrogant, although certainly weirdly fired up. There was something about him he couldn't fathom, something out of synch. He was beginning to think that he could talk forever, when there was a rattling at the front door. It slowly creaked opened to reveal an elderly woman, looking startled by Leon's presence. She stood for a moment, before approaching Greta for a hug, then peering suspiciously at Leon while peeling off her cardigan.

Quickly intervening, Greta introduced the woman to him, justifying his presence by explaining about the logs. But the woman interrupted, berating Pietro about something while pointing at his schoolbooks and the work-chart displayed on the wall. In an attempt to placate her, Pietro picked up and showed her the book on the Milan Museum, talking excitedly about it. But the woman only muttered and shook her head, taking the book from him.

If the boy had picked up on his grandmother's ambivalence towards Leon, he didn't show it. And as Leon pulled his jacket from the back of his chair, Pietro turned to him with a smile, warmly thanking him for his visit and for showing him the logs.

The cathedral was a riot of colours, styles, symbols and images. It was teeming with tourists. For Leon, it proffered scant appeal as a place where he might find peace, but at least it offered escape from the glare and heat of the sun. Greta searched for the resident curato, discovering him chatting with a group of flower arrangers. The man took them down into the crypts, and along a dark passageway leading towards the archivist's quarters. Leon was reminded of the one leading into the courtroom where Maria's inquest took place. That very first day – everyone sombre and troubled. He couldn't and mustn't go back to that; he wouldn't.

The woman Greta introduced him to was spindly-looking, yet sprightly and alert. She seemed excited to be receiving the logs. Setting them aside, she invited them to sit around her desk, before reaching for some box files from a side table, and laying them down in front of them.

"So, Signore Leon? We talk about your Benghi monk and the Order, the building now your hotel? It was a scandal of a place, as a child I heard it – all the gossip, all the anger. But my English – it is poor to explain to you."

Greta stepped in as translator. Once speaking Italian, the archivist became more animated, embellishing her story with colourful gestures. Every so often Greta held up a hand to signal her need to translate. Leon sat transfixed, learning how 'his' village was divided by this scandal. Newspaper clippings, residents' statements, transcripts of interviews with affected families, all showed how many believed their sons had been taken by the devil, others that they were pagans, casting spells and worshipping nature. But many found nothing wrong with the place: their sons seeming happy enough, allowed more freedom than in more traditional orders. But many parents felt robbed of the status that a more traditional role for their son would confer. Church authorities lobbied to have the place closed.

The Order grew plants and herbs for medicinal purposes, and these circulated amongst the community. Over time, many people came to believe the Order was protecting the fisherman, women in childbirth, everyone's overall health and wellbeing. The oil was distributed more widely as more people came to believe it its special powers, imbued by its makers worshipping their surrounding land and trees. This story, thought Leon, would have intrigued Maria. A tightness gripped his chest.

The curator went on to explain that for a long period of time, the Order was tolerated, and Benghi became the lead monk for gardening and training novices to the work. But a whispering campaign continued to simmer. In 1864 the Monastery was set on fire; there was one fatality, but part of the building and many of the trees escaped damage. No-one was found culpable, the site was abandoned, and the Order moved to Naples. The church wanted the site, but a charismatic benefactor stepped forward and redeveloped it as an ecumenical retreat.

"Little was known about him," Greta continued. "But rumour ran thick, suggesting he was running away from something. He managed the place almost singlehandedly, so closely and successfully that after his death, they could find no-one to succeed him. So, the Catholic church acquired the site as an administration and training centre. You know the rest – it was sold into tourism."

"Thank you, Greta." The woman smiled and turned to Leon. "Him, the man, the benefactor. He was a mystery man. He came – I think you have these words for it? Out from the blue."

Leon nodded. He was intrigued by the charismatic benefactor, and he had warmed towards his relative Benghi, a man who seemed to go against the tide.

"But alas, Leon," said the woman, removing a document

from one of the boxes. "It is sad, but you must both read this, it is important. Greta – is my word correct – obituary?' She handed it to her. 'You will translate, please? Then it is for Signore Leon, he can keep, it is a copy and I made it."

Greta read silently, then looked up at Leon. "Oh dear, Leon. It's Benghi. I'm sorry to have to tell you that he was the person who died in the fire." She handed the document to him.

As Greta drove them away from the cathedral, Leon kept a hold of the obituary, berating himself for not having mastered Italian. Greta had explained that it didn't say much about Benghi but there was some background information about his family, and she'd type a translation for him. He began to think about history, and how it might have its place. He thought about Pietro, how he would be interested to learn everything they'd been told, and wondered why the boy's grandmother disapproved of him giving him that book. He and Greta mulled things over, Leon more relaxed than he had been for some time. He asked her about Pietro's trauma and how she had tried to help, but Greta was guarded in her response.

Something about her kept reminding him of Maria. The dimples, perhaps? The way she glanced up at the sky or the ceiling, when thinking what next to say? Maria would be twenty now, half way through stage school, planning some project no doubt, probably in a relationship. He started to talk to Greta about her, how free she was as a child, how she loved the outdoors, the sea shore especially, the dunes, the cliffs. He disclosed how raw his loss was, how his anger could still erupt. His resentment at losing a child; why did it have to be them? Why did everything have to capsize in that way – just when he'd got his life well set up, won success on the stage? His anguish, witnessing the way she was killed. How she must have known it was G, the man who'd been hounding them.

"Wait . . . you mean it wasn't an accident?"

"It wasn't. She was murdered."

"Oh . . ." She was braking as she approached a lay-by.

"No – keep on driving, it makes the telling easier for me." Sweat was breaking out at the back of his neck, and he was almost hyperventilating. But the words kept tumbling out. "It was my fault you see – because I should have been able to stop it. A man with my standing, my money, I should have been able to protect them. I saw it all, Greta, you see I arrived just as he left them for dead . . ." He halted, wanting to retch.

"Hang on Leon, slow down. What do you mean it was all your fault?"

"He was in the audience. Unstable. I should have found a way to stop him."

Greta kept saying it wasn't his fault, he wasn't to blame, but he'd heard all this before.

"But listen, Leon. You don't blame Pietro for the drowning, do you? You'd never suggest that was his fault."

Look put up his hands. "That's not the same. I mean, the child wasn't killed deliberately, it was all a horrible accident . . ."

"Leon – take a look at yourself. You need to work things out here."

He shrugged; yet another person without a clue. He thought of his constant vigilance back home; looking for shapes in the shadows. And even out here he still sensed things lurking around. Just a glimpse of them, and then they dissolved. And he thought of his own well-honed powers, mocking them. His powers of hypnotism, engagement, mesmerising whole theatres of people. What good were they then? What good were they now?

| 4 |

Brushing his teeth the next morning, Leon thought about his dream. He was at the hotel, except its familiar surroundings were peeling away to reveal an earlier identity. It wasn't a hotel any longer, it had reverted to the days of the Order. The umbrella tree stood alone, freed of its dining room surroundings. But something was chafing, and he realised he was the one wrapped up in plastic, with only his head and feet spared. A lower branch of the tree reached out to touch his cheek, and the plastic began to unravel and fall away. I'm free, he shouted, for the very first time in my life, I am free.

He puzzled over this as he continued brushing. He was free, wasn't he? At least he was feeling calmer these days – well, most of the time. And meeting the boy had lifted his spirits, sharing the news about Benghi and the hotel.

He was the last to be finishing breakfast when Raphael approached him:

"May I speak with you Signore?"

"Of course."

"Signore Leon, I wish to be thanking you for your visit and kindness to my son. You see I worry about him, he is on his own, just sometimes he might see a friend, and each day his grandmother. It seems to me he can talk to you, it seems he trusts you, because he tells me this." He paused, looking anxiously at Leon.

Leon warmed to these words. "I'm so glad to hear that, Raphael. I enjoyed chatting to your son very much. It was a pleasure to spend time with him, he is a fine young man, a good soul. Any time you want me to call, and try and cheer him up, I will be happy to do so."

"Ah, but you'll be leaving soon, yes? It could not be good that he comes to depend on a friendship with you. This is agreed?"

He was surprised to hear this. "As it happens, I shall not be leaving soon. I have an open ticket and plan to stay for quite a while longer. And, if I were to see more of him, I would encourage him to get involved with the outside world, and not to depend on me. That could be a help to you both, don't you think?"

Rafael nodded thoughtfully. "You make some sense. But I would like to know from Greta – to see would she agree? She has given much to him, always kind, always thoughtful, always big hearted? I respect her judgment. So, you will ask her, yes?"

"Of course."

"And then Greta must let me know what she says to you."

Leon got up from his seat and clasped the man's shoulder. "Your Pietro – he's had a troubled time of it, and it must have been hard for you too. So please – I'd like to try and help, if you will allow it."

Raphael nodded. "I thank you, Signore."

But Leon thought the man looked uneasy.

He phoned Greta later that morning, surprised to hear her say she'd rather talk to him face to face about Pietro. She arrived after lunch, and they sat on the bench at the front of the hotel, her tone of voice quite firm.

"You said on the phone you think you can help to take Pietro out of himself and away from his sense of guilt. But Leon, ask yourself, should it be you doing this? I mean, you're still struggling with guilt yourself, aren't you? Look, it's fine to want to do some good for Pietro. But there's a risk, don't you see, that you might say something, unintentionally of course, that might make things worse?"

The new zest in his heart was evaporating. Hurt lurked in its place. She went on to talk about their working relationship, suggesting the boundaries were getting blurred, but that the fault was probably hers, as it hadn't been professional to take him to Pietro's house.

Leon was surprised at this, he expected people working for him to share his perspective. This was a different Greta today, and he felt quite wary of her. "Blurred? Well, isn't this conversation a bit blurry? And as for boundaries, aren't you stepping over one by bringing my personal life into this?" He imagined Kay chastising him at this point, reminding him of how he could be over-suspicious, expecting the worst of people. But shouldn't people earn your trust?

"Oh dear. It's a pity you have to see it like that, Leon."

"Well, maybe the best thing here is for us to leave it at that just now. But I will go away and think this through."

"But you've hardly given us time to talk about it properly, have you? I'd hoped we could make a decision today.

Still, if that's what you want, we'll resume our chat another time."

"And you're saying I'm not to see Pietro meanwhile?"

"Well, of course."

She sighed and turned towards her car. He walked away feeling deflated, it was not the kind of conversation he was used to having. Back in his room, he collected some beers from his mini bar, and placed them inside his backpack. Briskly crossing the car park, he headed towards the path at its rear – a shortcut, he'd heard, to the hillside and up to the village.

He rapidly climbed the path, kicking roughly at stones and debris, ignoring the sucking sounds of the sea, the hues and the scents, irritated by the mewing of gulls. Once or twice, he stumbled and cursed. He was thinking – wasn't he entitled to something better from Greta? He paid her well, and had been more than decent to her. His mistake had been the other day when he'd started talking about himself, letting everything spill out. She must think he was too unstable to be any good around the boy.

He turned his thoughts to Benghi, imagining the upset around his death, wondering if he'd maintained his connection with the village, and if he had also staggered up and down this path. Did he witness the same sights and sounds? Those great stones looming down at you? He supposed he also suffered anger and frustration. He wondered what it would be like to be Benghi in that emotional state, climbing this path, robes swinging to the rhythm of his pace, trying to calm himself down, telling himself not to unfairly judge people.

The vigour of his climb was starting to help, his breathing now deeper and slower, his thoughts about Greta kinder. But he'd strayed away from the main route and had to backtrack, re-crossing a stream where he paused to drink from the peaty water. His anger had died down completely, in its place a lonely weariness.

A longing for his daughter broke through. He sank down onto the side of the path, surprising himself by starting to weep, reaching into his backpack for his beers. Once his sobbing subsided, and his bottles were drained, the still and silence of the hillside felt comforting. Insects played around, and he could just make out the distant chug of a container ship. But there was something else – the sound of rustling and squeaking. A ball of fur cartwheeled towards him, halting and ridging to twice its size; in pursuit, a feral-looking mother cat. She plucked the kitten up, gave Leon a menacing stare, and retreated backwards into the scrub.

He wondered what Pietro's mother had been like. Protective? Playful? Affectionate? And what of Raphael as a father? Was he giving, was he nurturing? Leon's father had been distant. Leon had tried to give Maria more, but now doubted he'd achieved that. Most of the time he'd been on tour, returning to catch up with domestic things, often stuck in his study preparing for some charity event or other. Or simply exhausted.

Back on the path and approaching the village, he noticed a group of birds circling high in the sky, and realised they were vultures. Searching for a kill, he thought, a fallen goat perhaps. Now on the fringe of the village, he imagined it through Benghi's eyes. One or two pigs in a pen, perhaps, some hens scurrying about, one already slaughtered and plucked for the pot to celebrate his return. He studied the buildings closely, wondering who built them and how, the mining of the granite, hauling it up here with the help of horses. Did families live here for generations? He wanted to know more. About the residents' daily routines, about their beliefs. Their means of survival, both material and psychological.

A dog was barking from behind someone's gate. Ignoring it, he strolled across the square and entered one of the bars for a beer, receiving a few suspicious glances, the barman's demeanour hardly signalling a welcome. It was an austere kind of a place, with little natural light, and benches set around roughly hewn tables. It was cool inside, and that felt good. But shouldn't he return to the hotel, and contact Greta? He'd thought the onus should be on her, but now he wasn't so sure. She'd erected a barrier; maybe he was the one who should try and surmount it.

The truth was that something had drawn him to helping Pietro, but he wasn't sure what. He'd tried to understand people's motives, characters and personalities, because it was essential to his job. But had he learnt enough about himself?

When he woke the next day, he was thinking about the tree. He'd heard it whispering as he was falling asleep, a gentle sound close to that of someone breathing. It seemed to enclose him, and make him feel safe.

His breakfast had been left outside his door. He'd arranged this in case Raphael had noticed Greta had met with him yesterday, and wanted to ask him about her response. Now he'd finished eating, he knew he must phone her and apologise. But on getting through to her, his words tumbled out in some disarray, and her acceptance of his apology seemed half-hearted. She agreed to come over early afternoon, on her way to visit a client, and they could talk some more. She would also try and arrange for them both to talk with Raphael afterwards.

She arrived before he'd finished his lunch, and was starting on a second beer. Joining him, she asked Raphael for a coffee. The man seemed to linger, but Greta avoided eye contact.

"Just to say," Leon began. "Before we move on to your more serious matters, how pleased I am with your work. It's so thorough and detailed, and the threads you've opened up are really interesting." He picked up a folder he'd propped against the leg of the table, pulled out a sheet of paper and passed to her. "Please could you also investigate these questions? I hope they make sense."

Greta raised her eyebrows: "*Our* more serious matters, Leon." But she scanned his list, here and there asking for clarification, querying his final item – establish who the charismatic benefactor was. "So that's the donor who funded the Ecumenical Centre?"

Leon nodded. "I'm curious."

"That's certainly possible, but I haven't the time or skill for an in-depth search. I can commission someone, but it will cost you . . ."

"That's not a problem. Please go ahead."

"I can cover the rest of your questions – you've picked some interesting ones."

"Good." He told her how he'd like them prioritised. And as he talked, he explained his interest.

"You've become more absorbed in the history, haven't you? These are important issues – you've sieved away the detritus, found some gems."

"You think so? Pietro seems keen on history too. And art. He showed a strong interest in the modern art museum in Milan. It's a shame he hasn't been there yet."

"He would have, if he'd been at school. They do trips there."

"His grandmother didn't seem that happy with his interest . . ."

"Nonna? – they call her Nonna. But why do you think that is?"

He was surprised to find her reflecting his question back. "She doesn't want him to get above himself? And she herself doesn't appreciate art or history?"

"She's being protective. Over-protective perhaps. But why?"

Leon wanted to shun this. It felt like being in a classroom. "Jealous? Wants him to herself?"

Greta smiled, pushing her hair back from her face. "You could look at it this way. Pietro lost a mother; Nonna lost a daughter. A kind of balance in how to deal with that has been struck between the two of them, she may not want you disturbing it."

"But it shouldn't lead to Pietro being over-sheltered. He needs freedom to be who he is, or wants to be."

She sighed, her head slightly to one side. "Yes. But we all need to tread carefully."

The way she was looking at him reminded him of Kay, searching for what he really thought, as opposed to what he was saying. "I only wish them well," he said. "If there's anything I can do, while I'm over here with plenty time on my hands, I'm happy to do it."

"And what might be the best ways to help?"

The question stung him a little. His instinct was to offer money, but he held back. "You'd be the better judge of that, you know the boy better."

Greta smiled, remaining silent, waiting.

"Well . . . to encourage him to go out more? Seek ways for him to get involved in new things, develop new interests?" He was worrying that he sounded unsure of himself. "Or I could just be another person who's there for him. Someone to chat to, bring him out of himself while he's sorting himself out."

"A father figure, perhaps?"

Leon shrugged. "He already has a father."

"And sadly, you've lost that role, haven't you?"

Leon startled. "You think I'm seeing him as some kind of substitute for my daughter?"

"I didn't say that."

"I hope not. Because I'd find that offensive – no one could replace my daughter."

"Of course not. But if you are going to see him, we need to establish some boundaries. Especially as my work is going to take me away for a while." She solemnly asked: "What do you think is important here?"

43

He remembered his conversation with Raphael. "I'd caution myself against developing a friendship which might make him over reliant."

"Agreed – that's insightful. Anything else?"

He felt slighted by this process. "I suppose . . . not to promise what I can't fulfil? Er – and turn up when I say I will? Make sure Nonna and Father know what's happening. Let them know of any serious worries . . ." He gave her a wry smile. "Be polite . . ?"

"All so important, thank you, Leon. You agree to take all of that on board?"

"Of course."

"But there's something else."

"There is?"

"You can't think what?"

Leon shrugged, shaking his head. He felt like a child. "What is it?"

"Okay. Well . . . it's your drinking, Leon."

"My drinking?" He threw his arms up in the air. "For Christ's sake, what is this, Greta? Some kind of inquisition? Are you now going to pull me up for the way I button my shirt, or pick my nose, or something?"

"Sarcasm; I never liked it . . ."

"But who's saying I have a problem?"

"Your over-regular intake hasn't gone unnoticed. When we went to visit Pietro, you were smelling of alcohol, plus on every time we've gone on a trip. Your drinking is none of my business, except when it comes to Pietro. No drinking in his presence please, or prior to meeting up with him. Okay? Understood?"

He was thinking of Kay, and how his drinking was one of

the reasons they were taking time out from each other. "By whom has it not gone unnoticed?"

She patted her chest with a forefinger. "I have noticed, Leon. So, do I have your word?"

He gave her a tight-lipped look. "Of course."

She picked up his list of questions.

"Good. Then when we've finished our genealogy, we can sign off our contract. After that, I'll be off to Milan."

He didn't like the thought of that. "But couldn't we spend more time together going deeper into the research? You don't need those extra clients, I could pay you double, treble, of anything you could earn."

Before he registered her scathing look, he knew he'd said a very wrong thing.

"Huh. Really, Leon? You're in the way of buying friendship? It's worked for you in the past, has it?"

"You're making me out as someone I don't recognise."

"And didn't your Robert Burns have something to say about that?"

"Ah – you like to read poetry, do you?"

She smiled. "Look – while I'm away, I'm going to be in touch with Raphael about Pietro. Meanwhile, his home schooling is all set up, plus arrangements for his therapy and other support. How long are you staying?"

"I have an open ticket."

"Okay. I'll probably see you on my return, then."

They met Raphael half an hour later on one of the secluded terraces at the rear of the hotel.

Now they were away from other guests, Leon noticed a relaxed and humorous side to him, and a certain intimacy with Greta – of the kind he'd seen between brother and sister. He guessed this had developed through shared concern about Pietro.

But he also saw an impatient side to him – impatience with his son's progress. A frustration that the boy wasn't out on the street with his friends, and wasn't agreeing a return date to school, even though the home-school liaison officer hadn't called for this. He had been off school now for three months. As Greta and Raphael reviewed Pietro's home schooling together, Leon could see that Greta had sussed Raphael out well, and worked out how to relate to him. Now that Leon had calmed down a little, he could see she was a good communicator and sharp reader of character. Direct, yes, but not abrasive.

"Well, this I like," said Raphael. "I like looking at progress with you, Greta. And to also know, as you go away to work elsewhere, that you think his progress is good, yes? And importantly, that you are happy for Signore Leon to come to my house, as help and encouragement to my son?"

Greta nodded.

"You are very sure about this, then?"

"I am, it is all good." She looked at Leon. "We are both happy about it. And we agreed on some rules."

Greta now proceeded to spell out exactly what was expected. Raphael listened closely, nodding away, especially on the mention of "no alcohol". Finally, Greta added three more things: not to invade the family's privacy, never to pass judgment on Pietro, and refrain from any form of discipline.

The next morning, while walking through to his breakfast, Leon discerned extra activity in the hotel. He didn't pay much attention though, still smarting as he was over yesterday, especially the confrontation about his drinking.

His regular table was right at the back of the dining room. This he'd chosen so as to minimise interaction with other residents. Sitting down there, he noticed a specially drawn up dinner menu propped up against the olive oil dispenser. He picked it up, finding it festooned with balloons and other graphic details, like a child's birthday party invitation.

So. Today was a local festival, was it? A 'friendship' day, some kind of saint's day, and the hotel was going to be celebrating it. Perhaps he should dine at the Port, then – or somewhere else for a change – he ought to be making some plans to explore the area more widely, especially now Greta was abandoning him. But as he finished eating, he noticed some people approaching. A middle-aged, smartly dressed couple, looking over his way and smiling.

"Forgive us, Signore, our interrupting, and so brazenly, one might say. I introduce to you my wife, Colette, and I am Bernard. How do you do?"

Leon stood up abruptly, and shook hands with them. "Good morning to you. My name is Leon, and how can I help you?"

"So now I will tell you." The man gestured to Leon's seat. "But please, you must sit down."

Bernard quickly explained that to enter into the spirit of the festival, no guest should dine alone. So, could Leon join them at their table tonight? They had noticed that the gentleman always dined alone, but tonight, for this festival, he must not.

Leon's spirits sank. He put forward several excuses, but each was summarily dismissed, no doubt the couple thinking he was simply being polite.

After agreeing and saying goodbye, Leon tried to find a way out of it. Feign sickness? Come up with some sort of an emergency? He sat there quietly sulking, chewing his fingers, an old boyhood habit. Then after a while, he thought – what harm could it do? At least his cover hadn't been blown, there was more than a small mercy in that. But another thought reluctantly crept up on him: having dinner with them might help slow down his drinking.

At seven o'clock that evening, he entered the dining room to find it lugubriously decorated. A guitarist and vocalist were setting up their equipment next to the piano. How long was it since he'd last picked up his sax? But he did still regularly play his piano. Seconds later he noticed some flapping of hands from across the room. Soon he was settled in between them, their table close to 'his tree'. At least, he said to himself, it would be looking out for him, no doubt identifying with his boredom.

"So, you're French?" Leon enquired.

"Yes indeed – from Bretagne," said Bernard. "It is funny, is it not, how we can guess each other's nationalities? We think we are unique, and then, as you say, hey ho! We're each a common-or-garden person after all!"

Leon laughed to himself at their use of the term, while nodding and smiling. The couple established their home as in Quimper, a small town in the Finistère region, before proceeding to ask Leon some questions.

"Unlike us," said Colette, "You are too young for retired. You come here I wonder, to take yourself away for a well-earned break from a busy job?"

Leon was always ready for such a question, going on to describe his job in terms of his earlier work as conjurer-comedian at family parties. He introduced some spice by mentioning a few more glamorous jobs with well-heeled people, then mentioned his piano gigs in local hotels. The usual questions fielded and answered, Leon deflected interest back to the couple, ascertaining that they were boatbuilders, still sailing the seas themselves, but less ambitiously.

"Our son and daughter work in the business," said Bernard. "It is good for them that we come here, so as to have a free rein running the ship, you know? Sadly, we return tomorrow."

The waiter arrived with their starters, just as the musicians were striking up with a number from Cabaret . . . *What use is sitting alone in your room* . . . Leon listened to these opening words of the song, thinking it was of far better use than sitting where he was right now.

Two carafes of house wine arrived at their table, one of white, one of red. Leon would have liked a red of his choice, preferably Turriga, but they wouldn't stock that here. He could order something better later . . . but maybe he shouldn't?

Bernard poured the wine; Leon added some sparkling water to his.

"So," asked Colette. "How have you spent your time here?"

Leon explained his genealogy project, sharing what he'd learnt about the hotel's history, explaining the Order's

49

relationship with the olive trees, but didn't use the 'whispering' word.

"Your enthusiasm for history shines through, Leon," she said. "You are whetting my appetite for it."

"Good. And may I congratulate you on your English?"

"Yes," said Bernard, "It is I know better than mine is."

Leon didn't contradict him.

They were interrupted by the rumpus of a waiter banging on a steel tureen with a spoon. The guitarist was strumming eagerly, the vocalist flinging herself into some popular operetta. Then Raphael appeared, kitted out in what Leon judged as a monstrously gaudy costume, strutting like a matador, balancing on high a gilded dish (with some skill, he had to concede) on which smouldered an enormous ribbed roast.

The same waiter was now clapping to the music and the beat of Raphael's marching, leading a line of his staff round the room, the head chef immediately behind him. Others followed in order of status. All the diners were clapping, Colette and Bernard enthusiastically, but Leon less so.

As the crocodile exited, Colette asked: "And you Leon, you have children too?"

Again, he was ready. "I do not, unfortunately. My partner, Kay, she fostered a child. Things were in place to adopt, but he died very suddenly from meningitis."

"Oh," said Colette, "I am so very sorry, the grief never ends when a child is lost to you. So tragic. And I, myself, I grieve my twin brother. It was this year, on January the seventh. An accident, on the skiing slope."

Self-inflicted lit up in Leon's mind, which he immediately berated himself for. He offered condolences, did his best to avoid cliched questions about twins, while his heart strayed to Maria, and the milestones she'd been robbed of reaching.

"So, were you and your twin brother very close over all those years?"

"We were indeed." She spoke at length about the affinity of twins and the sudden twist of becoming an only child. Leon listened, pondering how the alcohol seemed to be flowing so very slowly, regretting not having discretely organised some chasers from the bar. He glanced at Bernard for signs of weariness or impatience with his wife. He found none, although the man did change the subject back to Leon's earlier delves into local history.

"It makes the significance of yourself seem very small," said Bernard, "When you are looking at that long grand sweep of everything that took place here in our hotel."

"You can feel that long grand sweep," said his wife. "It gets under your skin. Because I have noticed something with this hotel. I think you call it – atmosphere. Something here is a signal to us that the hotel is listening to us, that it has something to tell us, it is as if it has secrets."

Leon caught Bernard giving her a pointed look, but on she continued, about how they came here once before but in November, the hotel celebrating a festival of the ancestors. Didn't Leon believe that our ancestors needed to reach out to us? That we should revere them, connect with them, learn from them? She also claimed that she sensed a tension in the hotel, a heaviness and a sadness, that it needed to breathe more freely and free itself from its past.

Leon laughed, hoping to make light of it. "Well, I suppose we can all hanker after our youthful days, hotel or not? And we can all get a bit carried away by stories of supernatural things, especially reading books such as *The Shining*, that one by Stephen King. Have either of you read that one?"

They hadn't, so Leon explained he was reading it right now. He explained the plot, outlined the main character and his drinking problem, told them about the man's son Danny and how he had the sixth sense.

"Well," said Colette, "I believe I have a little bit of that shining in me. And, you, Leon, do you not feel it stirring in you? I am picking up on it."

"Colette," cautioned Bernard, "I fear you have taken too much wine." He shook his head at Leon "This is about much something and nothing, a piece of her nonsense l am afraid . . ."

"Bernard – what do you know about any of it? Leon – he knows nothing, I can assure you. And I can tell you, I am already wanting to read that book . . ."

Leon was searching for some way out, when he noticed Bernard catching their waiter's eye. The man started walking over towards them.

"Ah yes, waiter." He clapped his hand on Leon's shoulder. "We have *un pianiste accompli* here, a performing pianist. He could bring some extra colour to our evening, do you not agree?"

"Ah, this is Signore Leon, is it not? Of course, our musicians always welcome a turn from a resident. Signore Leon, you must follow me, please . . ."

Relieved at his chance to get away, he weaved between

tables, following the waiter towards the guitarist. He thought of that time he and Sue first played together, he on sax, she on clarinet – a Reinhardt number – they were at school. He recalled her flushed face as she looked away self-consciously, but still hanging around afterwards hoping to speak to him.

They swiftly agreed three numbers, established which keys, and who would solo. Warming to the task, he surprised himself with mastery of his chords, use of augmented sevenths and key transitions – he even sang a few lines of the final song's middle eight. Standing to acknowledge an appreciative audience, he was tempted to tell a few jokes, even deliver some tricks. But he desisted, keener to seize his chance not to return to the couple's table. Approaching their waiter, he arranged for him to make apologies to the couple, explaining he must make an urgent phone call. Then he slipped outside.

He gasped at the intensity of the densely scattered stars. The air was delicious – cool and sharp – the grasshoppers chirping away as if in celebration of it. Then he saw movement behind the azaleas. His fear returned as he recalled his lawyer's words: celebrities always end up with enemies.

Hurrying on, taking the path round the side of the hotel, he inadvertently came across the emptied lily pond. He backed away, thinking about the other drowning, the man he could only think of as 'G', throwing himself off that bridge.

Two days later he and Greta made a final visit together to see Pietro. In anticipation of this, he'd abstained from any alcohol. He could stop any time, he reassured himself, thinking that proved he couldn't have a serious problem. He had drunk too much in the past, that was true – in the days when Sue and then Kay were making their objections. But he had a reason then – it was because of Maria's murder.

Seeing Pietro lifted his spirits. Greta gently went over the ground rules with the boy. She was taking no chances then, of this Leon was clear. He sensed a poignancy to their goodbyes: Pietro was clearly fond of her, and there was a strong connection between them, but not a motherly one. Leon surprised himself here – he'd never much reflected on people's relationships. In a way he was glad Greta was going, because now he could establish his own territory. And he reckoned that, in spite of her ground-rules, there was still scope for manoeuvre.

A few days before she left for the north, Greta called at the hotel while he was down at the Port, to give him a file of the further research she had done. He stayed up into the early hours pouring over the material. Amongst other things, it built up a picture of the way the village functioned while Benghi was growing up there. There was also some material about the hotel when it housed the Order, including some photographs of the internal cloister, a basement library close to where his own room was, a group of habit-clothed men working in the olive groves, and a shorter and younger looking umbrella tree. There were some notes on its life as an Ecumenical Centre, with some information on the mysterious benefactor who'd helped to fund it. She'd passed her own copy of the file to a colleague, negotiating a fee for him to proceed with further investigations.

Lying in bed that night and mulling her findings over, some of the most salient surfaced and prevented him from getting to sleep. Most intriguing was Greta's suspicion that the anonymous benefactor had arrived under a forged identity, building a new life for himself in the fishing port.

Sleeping eventually, as the light of morning began to leak into his room, he dreamed again about the hotel as it might have been in the days when this benefactor was managing it.

| 5 |

Pietro's home schooler was packing her things away as Leon arrived on his first solo visit. Nonna, Pietro's gran, was skulking around the kitchen, having given Leon a lukewarm welcome. He'd waved and smiled at her, but there was little else they could exchange, as she spoke no English.

He'd brought Pietro a box of playing cards, and for Nonna, some flowers from the market, which she neglected to put in water. He managed a stilted chat with the home schooler, who brought to his attention some art work Pietro had been immersed in that morning.

"It is good, yes?" she asked.

Leon was astonished by its quality. "*Perbacco!* It certainly is, well done Pietro!" He enthusiastically patted his back, pleased to have picked up the Italian word for 'wow'.

What Leon saw was an abstract work of competing textures, with vibrant colours of ochre and violet. An uneasy and troubling unity had been achieved, suggesting an originality and confidence that was almost unbelievable in someone Pietro's age.

"Much more than good, yes?" said the home schooler. "So please – I'd like for some help with him and the art. Greta was saying he need this, too. It is also – Greta say, therapeutic. I know someone, someone good, for the art and for the therapy in it. But it costs, you know?" She pulled off her backpack, and picked out a business card from her purse. "Here."

He took it: "I shall look into this."

After she left, he pulled out his playing cards. "Want to learn a trick or two, then, Pietro?"

An uncertain smile crept across the boy's face. But soon, he was engrossed: "Where did that disappear to? Is it properly magic?"

Leon laughed, saying he had to obey the magicians' code and keep his secrets to himself.

"Things can come and go away in real life," Pietro said.

"Oh?"

He nodded. "Have you not seen that happen? Things other people do not see. And something, it makes you know that things are there, even when no-one can see them."

Leon felt wary, hesitating before replying. "I have not seen that. But I do have one or two tricks that I can teach you, ones that are not covered by the magicians' code. Would you like that?"

The boy nodded vigorously; Leon promised to order the props he'd need. Meanwhile, he pulled out the cones he still had in his pocket, and played the trick he'd shown to Greta.

Pietro watched keenly for a while, but then looked away. "Magic can never bring back what you want to come back, can it? Or make stay away those things you will hate forever?"

"I know," he said, "I wish it could." He wanted to comfort the boy in his expression of grief, but was mindful of Greta's ground rules. "Life can be cruel, and the bad things in life are not shared out fairly."

On his way back in his taxi, he thought of the parallel world of *The Shining*. A family stuck in a closed down haunted hotel, too frightened to use the lift. The sculpted topiary animals, coming to life. And a traumatised boy, burdened with the sixth sense. He felt good about the connection he had made with Pietro today. But as Leon watched the terraces with their heavily fruited trees speed by, he experienced a fleeting sense of dread.

He went on to see Pietro once or twice a week. The conjuring tricks arrived, and they practiced a few of them. He checked with Raphael and confirmed his agreement to art therapy sessions being paid for by him; an arrangement was soon in place. The father had seemed happy enough, if wistful that he hadn't been the one to recognise his son's talent for painting.

Out of this growing relationship emerged some faltering

chats about the surreal, and the boy's expressed beliefs in angels, saints and spirits. The conjuring tricks were of much appeal, Pietro developing a solid level of skill. He started to challenge Leon, wanting to know why he'd wasted all that expertise by giving up his job. Leon told a few half-truths, giving one as his desire to focus seriously on his genealogy.

"So," Pietro queried one day. "You are part Italian, and your family once lived here. That is why you are learning the local history. But you cannot be really living it, can you?" He smiled up at him, but in an accusing kind of way.

"So, your meaning, Pietro, is?"

"That you are here, in my country, and in your veins, there runs Italian blood. But you are speaking English still, and you rely on me – a boy – to speak in English to you. Where is your pride, that you have not enough inside of you to need to learn Italian yourself?"

"And," he went on, "I do not know if your story about your reasons for coming here, is the whole of the story. And then there is your reason for being here with me, helping with my art work, teaching me your tricks. It is not only to please Greta, or to please my father, I am thinking. Is it, I am asking myself, because you feel sorry for me? Is it to try and feel good about yourself, by trying to rescue me?"

"Rescue you?"

He nodded. "And is it also to seek ways in which to rescue yourself?"

He felt chilled by this, deciding that Greta or Pietro had been talking to the boy.

"You've got me there, Pietro! Something to think about.

And would you like to be rescued? Do you think you need that?" Leon was already reaching for his coat.

"No thank you," said Pietro, "It is better that we rescue ourselves."

After making some enquiries, Leon found just the person to help him, a peripatetic Italian teacher called Carlo, who would come to the hotel to teach him Italian. The lessons went well, and Pietro was keen for Leon to practice on him. After a couple of weeks of this, Nonna began to hang back, pleased to witness a few of Leon's wavering words of Italian, and offering a few phrases back. Initially, Leon captured little of the drift of what she said, even with Pietro's help. But after a few more weeks he felt confident enough to actively seek her out for one of their 'chats', which she now seemed to welcome.

Sometimes, when Pietro was using the bathroom, or making himself a snack, she would discretely approach Leon, keeping her voice low, having a few words with him: "This boy needs to go out more, don't you think?" . . . "Pietro needs to visit his friends". . . "He must go and visit the library, see his family up the mountains – Leon – you tell him . . ."

He would say to her "*Capisco che ci proverò Nonna*" – "I understand, Nonna, I will try."

But he was partly relieved of this by the arrival of the art therapist, who soon managed to coax Pietro outside to paint from life. The boy's resultant repertoire astounded Leon,

Nonna and his therapist, the latter providing a range of mate-
rials, helped by Leon's nod to an open-ended budget. This
included many art books, further fuelling the boy's skill and
imagination, and triggering an interest in the Avant-Garde.
He favoured the geometric shapes of Mondrian and Malevich,
and the exuberance of Kandinsky. He experimented as much
with their use of colour as with their composition, steering
himself into abstraction and symbolism. Alongside this, he
still maintained some interest in realism.

Asked to attempt a portrait of himself as he imagined
others saw him, he produced a cubist-styled head and shoulders, but with shards protruding from the eyes and neck, as
if he'd escaped from some war zone. In the background several hands were raised. Were they pleading for protection?
Signalling the viewer to back off? A later piece was a pulsat-
ing collage of colliding shapes and colours, all competing for
dominance. This painting was violent.

Sometimes, when Leon viewed a new piece of Pietro's
work and gained a sense of what it signified, he had an urge
to try his own hand. It was a strange feeling, as if there was
something needing to break out of him.

He made a habit of briefing Raphael about every visit, prais-
ing Pietro warmly and identifying landmarks in his progress.
The boy's father thanked him politely for his interest and his
time. But his responses erred on the chilly side, and he
refrained from indulging Leon in his head-waiter flourishes
at table. On leaving the dining area each morning, Leon
always paused to whisper to the tree: *La Luna, oggi vado a
trovare tuo figlio, ti saluto* – "La Luna, I'm off to see your boy

today, I'll say hello for you." Or sometimes: *Leri ho visto tuo figlio e sta bene* – "I saw your boy yesterday, and he is well." Each time he did so, he thought he detected a shiver of approval travelling down the tree's trunk.

He still went down to the Port, sometimes on the way to see the boy. But he no longer stopped for his daytime beers, mindful of Greta. Occasionally he had word from his agent, confirming rejection of another job offer. It was an expensive way of closing the door on things, but he wanted a gate keeper who knew him well, and could meet his needs. Each time the phone rang, he hoped it would be Greta, but several weeks passed and it never was. Raphael said he had heard from her – Greta's way, Leon supposed, of keeping a check on him. He'd also heard she'd been in touch with the home-school worker and the art therapist.

One June day, while Leon was helping Pietro with his calculus schoolwork, a friend called. It was a public holiday, and there was a carnival in one of the outlying towns he wanted to take him to. To Nonna's surprise and delight Pietro agreed, but with some reluctance. The next time Leon called, Nonna said the trip had gone well, with Pietro's usual waves of anxiety not once spiralling into full-blown panic attacks, or runs of flashbacks.

This heralded the planning of more ambitious ventures, including a daylong taxi trip to the mediaeval town of Salerno. Pietro had been pleading to visit its Giardino della

Minerva, a botanical garden he had learnt about at school. Leon and Pietro set off by taxi early one midsummer morning. The driver gallantly tried to give them some background on the way. But Pietro soon interrupted him in Italian, enthusiastically naming many of plants we would be viewing, and explaining the ancient system of canals and cisterns that brought water from the mountain springs. It pleased Leon to find Pietro animated and unfazed. He could just about follow his Italian as he talked about the architect of the garden, Doctor Matthew Silvatico, and his trips abroad in the Middle Ages to source medicinal plants.

Arriving in the town, Leon wanted to linger in its ancient parts and visit doctor Matthew's medical school – the first such institution in Europe. He was in envy of the doctor's legacy, but Pietro's impatience was palpable.

So, they headed for La Giardino, climbing up through the old terraces that stretched up from the river Fusandola. Finally reaching the top of a narrow flight of steps, they entered through a door in a high wall. The terraces continued throughout the garden, housing over two hundred species. Pietro readily identified the hallucinogenic mandrake, the *colocasia esculenta* (rich in antioxidants, he explained), and the ginseng.

"These three plants were all recorded in Benghi's logs," he said. "It is probable that he learnt about them be making visits here."

The boy stood for a moment, looking around him. It was quiet and still there, except for busying birds and insects. Enormous expanses of ocean and the ancient parts of the city stretched out around them.

"We must take it all in, Leon. The sights, the sounds, the smells. We must allow it to make a peaceful place inside of us."

Leon said he would do as he was asked, allowing his shoulders to loosen, his breathing to slow, while waiting for something inside him to expand.

"Do you have ambitions to be a guru or something like that, Pietro?"

"But can't you feel something?"

"Feel what?"

"The essence of this place. You know that word, don't you?"

"Are you talking about the plants?"

"I am talking about the essence of this place, this garden. I am calling your attention to what lies at the heart of it. The heart of its past, of its being. Can't you feel it stirring, rising up?"

He might be feeling something. The garden of the past somehow reaching out to him, drawing him away from his present. It felt akin to the way he used to be drawn into that old conjuring self, a self he happily escaped into, his very own world of rituals and smokescreens, a place to feel safe.

On their way back Pietro asked Leon why he never drove a car.

"The last time I did, something bad happened. I haven't been behind the wheel since."

"You are speaking here of the murder?"

"Of what?" Leon's back stiffened. "You know what happened to us?"

"I heard Greta telling my father. I have been wanting to say sorry about it." He hesitated. "Like me and the lily pond – a bad thing happens. Your life goes foul, like milk turns sour."

Leon was trying to temper his anger at Greta. "It does. But not for ever. You and me, we are going to be okay, don't you think? We're surviving, we're doing new things. It's not as scary, as upsetting as it used to be, knowing the one you lost can never join in with the things you do. Feeling disloyal, somehow – about leaving them out."

"Is it that? Like you must be abandoning them?"

"Yes. Like turning your back on someone you love."

"And the fear that it leads to forgetting them?"

"Exactly that."

"He was a sweet little kid." Pietro's tears were starting to spill. "I helped to look after him, those times when his mother and father wanted a break." He was trying not to sob. "I still see it happening inside my head, I can't stop it. It is the worst kind of hurting, hurting about something that is all your fault."

The remains of Leon's anger morphed into anxiety, triggered by thoughts of Maria's death. He placed his hands upon Pietro's shoulders, gently shaking them. "Look at me, listen to me, and believe what I have to say to you, Pietro, will you?"

The boy turned round, and nodded uncertainly.

"I want to tell you that it's not your fault. It is not your fault. *Non è colpa tua.* So repeat what I'm telling you. Okay?"

He nodded. "*Si Leon. Non è colpa mia.*"

But Pietro's voice failed to carry conviction. Everything felt close and clammy; Leon opened more buttons on his shirt. He then had a thought, and said: "The inquest into the drowning must have concluded it was not your fault?"

"I was not there, and Nonna and Father could not talk about it. I was not allowed to see the report, and Father destroyed the newspaper about it."

"Had you wanted to go to the inquest?"

"Of course."

After a week or so, Pietro had mastered most of the tricks, practicing on Nonna and some of his friends who called round from school. He began to relax more with them, and sometimes ventured out with them.

"When I make things disappear in the tricks," he said to Leon one day, "I am wishing for other things to disappear as well."

"You are? What things?"

"The things of real life." Pietro's voice was thinning, his eyes tightening. "The bad things, the horrible things, the things I see in my head. Like the lily pond, with his hair floating in the water, and hearing the sounds again – the shouts, the screams of his mother and father, the noise of splashing. And the biggest bad thing of every day is to wake up and find I am here, in that horrible place of knowing that he is dead."

"Yes. That must be the very worst thing by far. But then we have to find a way, don't we – not to be at peace with it, for that is asking too much – but to learn how to live with it."

"How do we make that happen?"

"How do we learn to live with it?"

Thus, began a time of exploring each other's stories, the darkest of feelings, the ways to try and deal with them. Grasping this freedom to talk about the one who died, about living with that pain of their absence. Learning how to live with that look in the eye of the person who's listening, but really thinking – *you must move on, get a life, keep quiet – because you're upsetting me, exposing my helplessness, making me realise I've run out of things to say to you.*

He discovered Pietro was attached to the village, and that he used to go up there from the back of the hotel. He was especially drawn to a ruined outhouse on the other side of it, a structure he said was quarried from camouflaging rock, a place to seek comfort, a place to do his thinking, cradled in the surrounding sounds and aromas.

Leon's Italian was improving – they frequently switched between the two languages, depending on who was struggling for the right words. Leon regularly asked Pietro about his art work, without saying that he personally had never been moved by art, not known what to look for, even wanted to try. He'd purchased his paintings, and there were many of them, at the request of his financial adviser.

"So how do you do what your teacher asked for – paint your feelings?"

"Emotions have different colours and shapes. They have smooth or jaggy edges, a quiet or busy look about them. They might explode, or put you to sleep."

"I see."

"You have to listen for them, feel for them, until you know which ones to use. But, Leon. You with your music, your piano and your saxophone. Do you not see colours for musical notes and for different kinds of melodies?"

He shook his head. "But you do?"

The boy nodded. "I know I am not weird or mad. I read about many people who see these colours. Painters, dancers, weavers, composers. And how they can go to a place inside themselves, like no other place that there is. This place, it is where you can be true, tell a thing in a new way, find a truthful way to say it." He studied Leon. "So, what about you, you with your conjuring, on your stage. You were making something, a thing of your own. Did that come from a different you, a place deep inside you?"

The question unsettled Leon. "it might have, in a way." But he knew that old escape route into his conjuring remained barred.

Leon continued to keep Raphael updated with some of the things he discussed with Pietro. Other things he left out, things he imagined Pietro may not want to share with his father.

"I know Father asks about things, asks about me, wants my progress. He wants me to have the life I had as before, but I cannot return, I am not that boy. And I cannot forget, so I am not pretending to anyone that I have or that I can."

Leon knew about that, all the pretending, he was good at it, and at holding things back. He'd told Raphael the truth about how his son was doing fine, getting out more, studying well and trying out new things. But not about the way they were talking, because he didn't want Raphael thinking he was trying to change his son, feed him ideas, teach him to think. He didn't want Raphael and Greta agreeing he was a bad influence.

One evening, on his balcony and reading the final chapters of *The Shining*, he unnervingly noticed some parallels. The boy with the father who can't help him. The man who comes through a blizzard, to rescue him. It made him question himself, now Pietro was finding new paths for his life. Why was his own life so stuck?

| 6 |

An art exhibition had opened in a local museum, and Leon had interested Pietro in it. They set off early one hot July morning, agreeing they'd picked the right day to spend time in a marbled interior. For a change at this hour, Leon was feeling good; yesterday's alcohol restricted to two small beers with his evening meal. He even tested his Italian on the taxi driver, but the man seemed in a negative mood, decrying the exhibition as elitist bullshit, especially the installations. He then went on to laud the work of a niece who painted portraits, berating how the museum had refused her exhibition space. Pietro told him the best kind of art was provocative, because it forced people to look at the world in different ways.

But they were both disappointed in the installations, agreeing they were a haphazard display of failed attempts at something novel. Only one thing appealed – a giant spider, made of reconstituted plastic retrieved from local beaches, its web engulfing most of a single room. They doubted it would have been quite so distinctive though, if it weren't for its scale.

Pietro was most absorbed by the abstract paintings, telling Leon what he thought the artist had achieved, who they were influenced by, how they'd used texture, colour and light. Whenever Leon picked out something he liked, Pietro wanted to know why. Watching him pacing around, Leon thought how much he'd changed, how he was now more relaxed and focused.

A painting by Umberto Boccioni caught Pietro's attention. He told Leon how this artist reminded him of Picasso, but he preferred Boccioni's work because it was warmer.

"Have you seen Picasso's *Guernica*?" Pietro asked.

"Yes. It's quite shocking, very forceful. It manages to present all the strands of what happened. For me, it truly brought home the brutality of war."

"My teacher said that you cannot appreciate that painting unless you have studied what happened in Guernica – the methods the fascists used to kill those people, how it was all a disgusting experiment in warfare. Do you think my teacher is right?"

"It must help to know something about the history. But the painting's power is in making people want to find out more. That way, it's become a prevailing memorial to those who suffered."

"My teacher is a snob about art."

"Hmm. You don't really like him, then?"

"He's okay, He taught me plenty of things. I have to try and like him, because he is a cousin of my mother."

Leon imagined that Pietro would soon surpass his teacher. The boy was already talking and thinking in ways that suggested he'd skipped a large chunk of his childhood. His English too was becoming more polished than ever.

Over lunch in the museum cafe, Leon asked Pietro about his mother.

"What was she like, Pietro?"

"She was tiny, with long black hair always falling into her eyes. She had a crooked finger that was broken playing tennis, and a little scar on her nose. She liked to hug, she liked to listen to what I had to say, she always answered my questions." He paused to blow his nose. "When she died, I was eight. I stole a scarf of hers that I found in a drawer, it still has her smell on it. I found some photos too. I look at them when I'm very happy or very sad. They say she was like me, always lost in her own thoughts."

"That's nice, I can't imagine anyone thinking I'm like my daughter."

"What was she like?"

"Tall and athletic, straight hair the colour of chestnuts. A strong voice, eyes that flashed; she could be funny, kind, sullen, generous, angry, driven, sometimes sarcastic. And she knew how to bring people down to size, especially me! She just enjoyed life, couldn't get enough of it."

"What age was she?"

"Older than you – seventeen when she died, three years ago. I miss how she made me laugh. It wasn't so much the things she said, but her way of saying them. Quirky."

"But Leon, you too can be quirky. You have much energy, and you can make me laugh. You might be more like Maria than you think."

"That surprises me."

Pietro nodded, returning to the subject of his mother, how his loss felt like a dark empty space, nagging away inside of him, wherever he was, wherever he went. How a struggle with a painting could feel like trying to paint her back into his life.

"Can you imagine what your mother's hopes for you might have been?"

He shrugged. "I have never thought about it."

"Well, try. And once you have, try and let them come alive in you, fill up that dark, empty place you spoke about."

Pietro stared at Leon. "But that is something you also should do. For your daughter."

"For Maria? I will try. But promise me, that in spite of your mother's death, you will build a good life, not just for her, or your father, or Nonna, but for yourself. A meaningful life, in which you believe in yourself and pursue your goals, and in which you find space for your art work."

Pietro sighed, but nodded.

On the way home, Pietro said: "I read on a plaque in the museum, some words of an American scholar, John Dewey."

"Oh?"

"It said: art is an attempt to find light in a great darkness. I like that."

They went on to debate the purpose of art. Was it to reflect the way the artist saw the world? Experienced the world?

Wanted to change the world? Or was it to help the viewer understand the world? Or simply for people's enjoyment?

Pietro started to giggle. "We'll never agree! But we enjoy disagreeing, we like having an argument!"

Arriving on the drive up to the hotel, Leon saw that familiar shadow of someone working amongst the olive trees, but it comforted him, somehow signalling that his life was getting better. And back in his room, as the tree sighed away in its usual style, he felt much better for his trip, and for knowing Pietro was getting the opportunities he deserved. He lifted the phone and made a call to his lawyer's office, putting in motion arrangements for a translated copy of the inquest report into the drowning to be sent over to him.

A few days later, enjoying a bowl of seafood soup for his lunch, an unfamiliar contentment settled over Leon. He was feeling almost as good as the best of times before Maria was killed. Perhaps there with something about coming back to his roots, and connecting with people outside the entertainment industry, people who didn't know him for his other self. How strange, he thought, to be this introspective – wondering about cause and consequence.

Looking up from his soup to glance across the dining room, he caught Raphael eying him sullenly. After finishing eating, he walked towards the lobby, only to find Raphael catching up from behind and asking for a word in the garden. They walked past the topiary and over to the pool – too early for residents to be hanging around there – and settled down at a table.

"Signore Leon, this is about Pietro," he began. "I have to say it to you, that I am grateful for what you have helped with. But, sorry, I think it is all too much. Like with the teacher you found and this arty painting stuff, I know it is called therapy, but I do not think I want it or like it."

In spite of the warmth of the sun on his back, Leon felt chilled. "But why, Raphael? It's made such a difference to Pietro; it's brought some life back into him."

Raphael shook his head: "But he has always had plenty life in him." He frowned, going on to say that he didn't want Pietro growing up with weird ideas, imagining a life beyond his station, thinking he's better than anyone else. Would Pietro's next thing be wanting to go away from his family? Would Raphael then lose him also, along with having lost his wife? Art was no vocation for a man. The right vocation would be the navy, the police force, or being apprenticed to a trade. Anything that assured financial security.

"But Raphael, shouldn't he decide for himself? He must take the best opportunities open to him, and he is very, very skilled in painting. His aptitude, his enthusiasm, and his capacity for hard work could take him a long, long way . . ."

"So, Signore Leon, which of us is it? Is it you or me, who knows him best? Who is the father, eh? I understand you lost your daughter, Greta has told me, and I am sorry for that. But are you wanting my son to now take her place? And you have money. Money talks, money wins influence. But it cannot, it will not, buy my son's friendship and his choices in life."

Leon stared at the man, surprised by this challenge, and struggling to understand it. "But Raphael, I had hoped that by helping Pietro, I was helping you, too. You did encourage me to spend time with him, you know."

"But you cannot – I think you say – gatecrash – a person's life. You must go and find a way to say to my son that it is all coming to an end. He is doing very well now anyway; he is doing a very lot better. And soon he will be starting at school."

"Will he? He hasn't told me that."

"You don't believe me? Huh. If so, you can ask the home school lady."

"Okay, Raphael, thank you. I believe you, and I think I understand you."

"I am glad to hear it."

Raphael told Leon he should make a final visit to his house, to say goodbye to Pietro.

A feeling of inevitability came over Leon as he returned to his room. Sadness clutched at him as he lay down on his bed.

The following afternoon, he went to see Pietro to tell him. But, arriving at his house, Nonna explained the boy was sick in bed with a stomach upset. Closing the door of the steep staircase up to his room, she motioned to a chair for Leon to sit down so she could talk to him.

The woman spoke in slow Italian, using short sentences and extravagant gestures for emphasis. She hesitated after each phrase, searching for signs that he was following her. The gist of it was that his trip to the museum with Pietro had done more harm than good. Their conversation had been unhealthy, there was no benefit to winkling out the boy's past, in opening up old wounds. It was selfish of Leon to have done that, and it had undermined Pietro's relationship with his father.

Her words cut into Leon, and an old ache started up in his back. He knew there was nothing he could say that would change her view of things, and she did go on to acknowledge that Leon had helped in some ways. She said he must come back once the boy was well, and say goodbye then.

He nodded. "*Grazie.*"

She smiled. "*Se vuoi aiutare, aiuta Greta. Tornerà presto a casa, credo, ma è malata. Una ragazza triste, una povera ragazza. Per essere utile! Chiedi a lei!*" . . . "If you must help someone, help Greta. She's coming home, soon I think, but she's sick. Ask her, make yourself useful to her!"

Back at his hotel, he anxiously rang Greta's number. He knew she wouldn't answer, but he left a message to say he'd heard she was on her way home, hoped her trip had gone well, that Pietro was much improved, and could they meet up once she was back. He didn't mention her health, for fear of being intrusive.

The next day Raphael approached him, saying that Nonna had said he could visit Pietro later that afternoon. Leon thanked him, saying he would, and asking after Greta. But Raphael said he had no further news, moving on to ask when Leon was returning home.

"It becomes too much heat, this time of year for tourists. You must need to be with your wife, anyway? After your absence of three months, she will miss you. Especially needing to share the sadness of losing your daughter."

Leon was shocked by the man's direct approach, quickly explaining that he and his wife were no longer together before making excuses to get away. After a brief walk around the gardens to gather his thoughts, his fingers still clenched and his chest feeling tight, he walked to the bus stop to make his trip to Pietro. His life felt suddenly changed.

By the time he arrived, he'd rehearsed what he wanted to say. But Pietro was back in bed after further bouts of vomiting. A neighbour was watching over him while Nonna was out shopping, citing food poisoning. She refused Leon's request to see him, passing on a message from Nonna's that he must say goodbye in a letter, but agreeing to give Pietro an art history book Leon had brought for him. Waiting at the bus stop, debilitated by the heat and his spirits low, the home school worker came by and said hello, confirming that Pietro was very soon returning to school.

"Signore Leon, I believe it is the art work that has given him back his life. You helped that happen, and he knows he needs to return to school to study it. His art teacher, he promised me that he will make special provision for Pietro." She smiled. "I know his father has spoken out against this to his boy. But that, I find, has made Pietro more determined!"

Leon laughed, going on to voice his disappointment at not being able to say goodbye to him except by letter.

"Well, write your letter for him, and send it to me. I will make sure for you that he receives it."

He made several attempts at the letter, frustrated at having to use this medium. With each draft, he was reminded of those other letters, the ones his lawyer had penned, and sent to G. The ones he should have insisted on having a hand in.

Dear Pietro

I hope you're now feeling better. I was saddened that your illness meant I could not see you when I called, but Nonna has asked me to write this letter.

You are now returning to school, and I'll soon be travelling back to the UK, so we must part ways. Hopefully now that Greta is returning home she will keep in touch with you, and send me your news. But today I want to thank you for our friendship, it taught me some things about life and opened up my mind.

I know you'll respond well to returning to school. You've kept your interests alive, and forged new ones which I'm sure will thrive. You're at a crossroads now, and it can be hard to listen to your inner voice, and weigh that up against what others want or need from you. I'm thinking of your quest to be a painter. But there are ways to listen and be answerable to both yourself and others.

Life is full of contradictions. Yin and yang. Will we grow, or will we wither? So much comes down to making sound choices and opening ourselves up to learning. To have a relationship with a craft, a skill, a creative endeavour allows an extra dimension into your life, one that feeds your spirit. If lucky enough to be favoured with that, a duty exists to nurture and cherish it. But I think you sense and know that.

I believe in you, and in your future.

With my warmest wishes

Leon

A fortnight passed, and neither Greta nor Pietro got back to him. Resigned to the likelihood of seeing neither of them again, he began planning his return to the UK. But the next morning Raphael informed him that Greta had been in touch to find out if Pietro had settled into school. He explained she was having some medical investigations, and had asked about him. So, Leon rang her, but she failed to pick up. In his message he said that he was soon to return home, and could he treat her to supper as a way of thanking her for all her help?

Two days later a handwritten note was dropped off for him at reception:

Thank you, Leon, but supper does not suit me; I have no appetite. Could we briefly meet for coffee to wind up the job? I'd also like to find out how you got on with Pietro. Unless I hear otherwise, meet me in Juno's café in the Cathedral Square Wednesday morning at 11:00, Greta.

When Leon arrived, the square was seething with tourists. But Juno's was relatively quiet, tucked away in a secluded alleyway, and they were quickly served. Greta's drawn complexion unsettled him, and he asked outright about her health.

"The doctors found a blood disorder. It's cancer, quite a rare one."

Her words numbed him. "I'm so very sorry. Have they caught it early?"

"Not really, but it's not as aggressive as some. If I can cope with the treatment, it could buy me a fair amount of time. There's nothing like cancer for making you focus on things you want and need to do. It might make you physically wrecked, but it gives you emotional drive."

This steely approach won Leon's respect. "Indeed. So, what are you planning?"

"Well – a mixture of practical things – with hopefully a few wild things thrown in . . ."

"Wild things . . ?"

She smiled. "I keep my wild things close to my chest, Leon."

He felt a bit slighted. "I might be able to help you, you know . . ."

She gave him a scornful look. "If it's money you're offering, forget it. I don't want to be on some charity list, just so you can get to feel good about yourself." She paused. "Oh dear, I apologise. Let me take that back – I'm on a short fuse, I guess. But, come on. Let's talk about Pietro. How did it go with him?"

Leon had worked out a response. "Happily. He's been getting out a lot more – with me and with friends. He'll be settled back at school now, and the art therapist – she worked wonders. He's developed a strong interest in art, and has a huge talent. Quite a shining light, something of a protégé, I'd say."

"I agree with you, he has exceptional creative talent and insight. But were there any difficulties?"

"Difficulties? Well, he wasn't too well a couple of weeks ago . . ."

"I know. But how do you think things worked out with Raphael and Nonna?"

"You've spoken to them?"

"Yes. It seems there were some things they weren't too happy about . . ."

"I suppose so. But Pietro was happy with my visits, I think . . ."

"He's clever for his age, Leon, you are right. But he's still too young to properly judge what's best for him. He's still a child, you know . . ."

"He doesn't behave like one, Greta. Or like a sulky pre-teenager, either."

"Being gifted and being adult aren't the same. He might be talented, yes – but he's too young to have much emotional intelligence."

"But he has needs. And they're different from how his father sees them."

"People's needs are relative. They're rooted in family, and in their community. You're looking at this through the lens of your own culture and background, Leon."

"Oh yeah. I suppose I come parachuting in, then, causing havoc everywhere and to everyone . . ."

"That's not the way I would put it . . ."

"So, who's to be the winner? Pietro and his needs, or his father's and Nonna's?"

"It's not a competition." She sighed. "Look, Leon, don't think I can't see your point of view. I've actually spoken to the home schooler and the art therapist, and they both speak well of you and the progress you helped Pietro to make. They do think you may have overstepped the boundaries a bit, but they don't think any harm was done."

"Oh . . . the boundaries . . ."

She shrugged. "Let's leave it at that. I do want to thank you – for being there for him, for bringing such a positive benefit – whatever Raphael and Nonna might think."

She diverted into talking about her trip, the difficult and the boring bits, the intriguing clients, her car breaking down in the middle of a cloudburst. She then checked her watch.

"We need to finalise things. Remember our mysterious benefactor? I've got quite a lot on him – and an invoice – it's going to cost you." She removed an envelope from a folder, handed it to him, then patted the folder. "There's a load of information in here. You'll see how the benefactor narrowly escaped being murdered in his town of birth. It was retaliation for something mafia related, he managed to escape under a changed identity, helped by the church, following a full confession. I've verified that his wealth accrued from a family inheritance built on profits from slavery.

"Bequeathing the money in the late 1880's for the Ecumenical Centre was a kind of penance for his links to slavery. An influence was his knowledge of the reformer and ex slave-trader, John Newton, and his forceful pamphlet. They shared the same birthday – 24th July, but of course a century apart. Newton repented his connections with slavery and joined the ministry, moving into a diocese in a small town called Olney, where he met William Cowper, who was a poet.

Together they wrote the hymn Amazing Grace."

"My goodness, that's fascinating, especially his obsession with Newton. I'd like to learn more about that."

Greta reached down for her briefcase, and pulled out a large sheaf of printout. "There's plenty more here. Take it, but none of it has been translated yet."

"You're forgetting something . . ."

"Oh?"

"That I've been learning Italian."

She grinned at him. "But of course. Good on you, Leon."

"I have a lot to thank you for, Greta. You've helped me understand some things – especially the value of history, and even some things about myself. Spending time with Pietro, that taught me things too. Watching him learn, thinking about how people learn, why they want and need to, how it affects other people. So please, allow me to help you, in the way of a thank you. There must be something you can suggest."

"I'm glad it's been helpful. But I don't want your money, Leon, I don't want to see your generosity listed in some charity journal or other, next to a photo of me."

He smiled in admiration of her. "Message received. But do me a favour, Greta. You say you keep your wild things close to your chest, but I promise you they'd be safe with me. I doubt you'll see me again – I'm leaving this place shortly. And I have a few wild things of my own I'm planning to release once I get home. So, let's do a deal here. If I let you have a peep at my wild things, will you let me have a peep at yours?"

Greta laughed. "When you put it like that, Leon, you might just get your wicked way with me."

Late morning, he took a taxi to Pietro's school and spoke briefly to the head teacher about a 'friend' who wished to set up an art fellowship by making an anonymous donation. The headmaster keenly set things in motion, providing the name of a trustees' chairperson, to whom such a request should be forwarded. Back at his hotel, he phoned the airline to confirm his return flight. Later, he went for a late afternoon stroll in the grounds, but it was oppressively hot, and most of the plants looked dry and straggly, well past their best. Walking towards the olive grove he heard the distant sound of rustling leaves, and there in the distance he picked out the figure of Pietro, partly hidden by a hedge, beckoning him.

"I shouldn't be here," he whispered, once Leon was beside him. It is my father's day off, and he thinks I am in the library. No-one must see me, or know I came here. We must find a hidden place."

While pleased to see the boy, Leon noted how troubled he looked. Pietro led him to a remote and neglected corner of the gardens, where they sat on a bank behind some shrubs, flicking at the insects. Perspiration glistened on Pietro's brow, and he sounded agitated.

"Thank you for your letter, it made me think about some things. But you have to help me. I am feeling all mixed up."

Leon held his breath – was all the progress being undone? "Just talk, Pietro, say anything, it doesn't matter how it all comes out."

"I don't know what to say, I don't know what to think . . ." He was now shedding tears.

"What is it? Tell me."

"I just feel bad about everything."

"Is it about the drowning? Do you still feel bad about that?"

"Sometimes, yes."

"Because I have something back in my room that could help you. Shall I get it?"

The boy sniffled and nodded, and Leon ran off quickly, returning with his copy of the inquest report.

"This is your copy, keep it. You have a right to it."

The boy flicked through the pages, crying, but nodding. "I am glad to see it, it helps that I see the writing, and that it is an authority which is saying all this."

"You have a right to this information."

Pietro folded the pages carefully before pocketing them. "I feel better – a little bit. But the letter you wrote, it made me ask questions of myself. I cannot be the boy I was, this place's tree whisperer. The land here that I loved, it feels unfriendly now, after the drowning, and after being away from it. And Father says the hotel soon will be sold, in any case."

"Will it? My goodness. I didn't know that."

"I want you to help, I want to feel better." He hesitated. "You wrote in your letter about the yin and the yang. This has helped you then, this philosophy. It is Chinese, is it not?"

"Chinese? I don't know, I'm really not sure . . ."

Pietro sighed. "What? You use an ancient saying, but don't care about its origins?"

Leon shuffled; he was uncomfortable sitting on the bank. "I suppose that's shameful . . ."

Pietro nodded. "But I have been finding it out – in the library. It means light and shade, negative and positive, two things that are opposites. There are all these forces, so you find the balance. And then I read about the Qi. It is the life force, the energy the world came from, something very important to Chinese medicine and philosophy . . ."

"Now I'm out of my depth. I only know the word Qi for playing a game called scrabble – it doesn't need a U after its Q . . ."

Leon paused hoping to see a smile, but gloom was settling over Pietro.

"Why should I bother discussing your letter, if you fail to know what you are writing about?"

"But we could still discuss the things it's raised for you?"

Pietro took a deep breath before exhaling slowly. "You wrote down that there are ways to listen and be answerable to both yourself and others. What you mean is, I can do what Father and Nonna want, and at the same time do what I want. But you do not explain a way to make that work, and I cannot find a way."

"It was just a turn of phrase, Pietro. But there are ways to resolve differences, you have to work at it, and it can it take time, compromise, discussion, some explaining. Most of all it takes listening, and tolerance. Do you see?"

"Not really. What use is that to a kid, surrounded by adults? I came up here risking my skin to talk to you. But you tell me those things that you wrote are nothing more than a turn of phrase. Was it the wine that made you write them?" Pietro's voice was wobbling now, becoming squeaky. He turned his head away to hide his tears. "You try to make me think it will be alright, don't you? But it won't be. They stopped you from seeing me, didn't they? They told me they think you are bad for me, that you put some stupid ideas in my head, and they tell me you are a drunk . . ."

He plucked some stones from the ground and started throwing them around, his tone getting angrier as he talked on. Vivid examples tumbled out, of difficulties adjusting to being at school – some students he thought were friends now ignoring him, others having made new friendships or joined a rival group. One such group had been pursuing him with taunts, asking if he'd been locked up in a *manicomio*. Others jeered that he was a freak, a weakling skiving off school with nothing wrong with him. Isolated, with no words of support from his teachers. The more he spoke, the more worked up he became. Leon's peace of mind was shredded.

"So you see? I am far from okay, I have panics again when outdoors, I have terror thoughts in my head. It feels as if a very bad thing is creeping around and following me every-where, getting ready to happen. There is one only place left safe for me, and that is up by the village."

Something had distracted Pietro, he was squinting at it through the branches, his body shaking. "Someone is coming. You must go back over there somewhere, and distract them. Please do this now, and then I can creep away along the bushes."

Leon woke well before six the next morning, in a state of deepening unease. By half past six he was being served his breakfast, but not by Raphael. This was a relief, but as he walked through the foyer, he heard the receptionist saying that Raphael's son had gone missing. Standing there in shock, he imagined he heard a snow plough whining. But it was only the umbrella tree busy whispering, this time more urgently.

His shock burgeoned into distress. Had he upset Pietro yesterday? Had the boy gone off because of something he'd said? He went outside and paced around the garden, then returned indoors to his room, to stare from the balcony at the volcano. His thoughts drifted back to the snow scene in *The Shining*, the driver of the plough trying to reach the imperilled boy, with hazard after hazard preventing him. The sound of that blizzard seemed to encircle him. But – no – it was the tree again.

Should he let Raphael know that he'd seen his boy yesterday? But Pietro would never forgive him. And suddenly he realised that if he did that, he could be identified as the last one to see the boy. He stared across at the volcano; it seemed to be sulking at him. Surely this thing with Pietro would turn out to be nothing? Maybe his father had overreacted to some minor act of defiance, triggering a teenage outburst and a brief hiding away. Or had Pietro been egged on by boys in school? Skiving off to some out of bounds remote café-bar, smoking a fag, fooling around, a bit of horseplay. But he knew the boy well now, and he was far from impulsive.

Back in his room, his phone was ringing. It was Greta.

"Leon – have you heard about Pietro?"

"Yes. Have they found him?"

"No. He's been missing since yesterday. You'd better watch out, Nonna and his father are saying it's all about a weird and interfering letter you sent to him. And someone saw you with him at your hotel yesterday."

"For God's sake. Do they think I'm some kind of pervo, or something?"

"Well, I'm sure they'll be using their imagination."

"Meaning?"

"You'd better have a good story ready."

He lay down on his bed to think, taking comfort in the tree. He felt anchored to this place now, and he imagined the roots of the tree must feed on everything that had happened there. He fixed on what he needed to do next, and was soon on his feet, seeking out some sturdier shoes. As he tied his laces while the tree grumbled away, he searched around in his head to find a way to make things better.

Passing the topiary as he hurried towards the village path, he caught sight of a privet clipped into the shape of a fish. A tremor was rippling through it, and in the watery light of morning he noticed a flicker of fins.

A breeze was stirring up the foliage on the hillside. He hardly noticed the familiar landmarks as he trudged on and up, weighing up his thoughts, the sun scooting in and out of the clouds, a flotilla of yachts competing in a regatta. So, the boy must be up here, the place where he said he felt safe, somewhere to help him take stock of himself and his life. Leon felt hopeful.

But, then – alone? Up there? Fears for the boy took hold again like a phantom's clammy embrace. He glanced behind him, his longstanding dread still wrenching. There was no-one, but his mind's eye filled up with bubbles, red ones, seething and spluttering. The roof of his cherry red Alfa

Romeo, foaming away in the acid, a motorcyclist speeding off. Not long after that, those words in a note pushed through his letter box: Death to your wife – please check the garden. A scarecrow structure, impaled in the turf, Sue's photo fixed to it with duct tape. A knife embedded in the creature's stomach, sawdust spurting from the wound. He'd yelled abuse at it, kicked it, stamped it to shreds, after removing her photograph and clutching it protectively.

He cursed as brambles clung to his ankles. Why would a boy disappear? No, it couldn't be that, he couldn't be wanting to take his own life. Yet maybe he's worse than you think – faking his 'wellness', pretending to be what folk want to see. Leon got that, he did the same, and wasn't he still doing it? Easier than being honest with those who want you better, want to find you reverting to your 'normal' self.

As he kicked at some stones at the side of the path, his fear punched in at a deeper level. His grief now unleashed, it churned away, dredging up flashes of photographs shown at Maria's inquest. The stump of her arm, a dislocated jaw, the blood splattered amongst the roses. Sue's many injuries as she tried to defend their daughter, her anguish caught in his headlights as he drove up their drive. He could still hear her screams, remember her nightmares.

Trudging on up to the final section of the path, the death scene began to dissolve. His grief now seemed to drain from him, becoming external, as if he were travelling up in a cliff lift, observing the grief itself lodged inside the returning car. He envisaged it gliding past him, lodged on its rails, unable to hurt him. Shaking his head at his own bizarre imagery, he reached for the latch on the gate in the fence at the point where the path led into the village.

The church bell began tolling, signalling a funeral. He set out towards the piazza, imagining Benghi returning for a visit, perhaps to help someone in need. He scanned the windows of the domestic buildings, wondering which ones housed people known to Benghi. All of them, probably? Crossing the piazza, he sought out the narrow lane that Pietro told him about, running from the end of the village and becoming an overgrown track. Once on it, and leaving the village behind, he spotted the rocky escarpment rising up from the land. But as yet, no signs of the ruin.

As the path took him into the scrub, a gang of long tailed tits rose up, disturbed from stripping insects from the growth. The sun was hidden behind low clouds which had gathered grumpily along the headland. His spirits low, he quickened his pace. Nearing the escarpment, he could make out a protrusion, a shade lighter than the rock, but smoother in texture. That had to be the ruin.

He slowed down, the track now smothered with tangled growth, and hardly discernible. If the boy was there, he mustn't frighten him by approaching unannounced. So, he began calling out to him. "*Pietro! Pietro! Sono io, Leon!*" Then he walked closer, all the time listening, watching, waiting, hoping. Nothing. Only silence. Then at last some rustling and scuffling, as a shadow appeared, transmuting into a sullen and bedraggled figure. And there stood Pietro staring in silence, before stumbling towards him.

Leon was awash with relief – as if sunk in a bath after scaling a mountain. He scrutinised the boy's face – it was grimy, and crumpled with fatigue.

"How did you know I was here?" Pietro asked grouchily as he neared him.

"Just a guess . . ."

Holding back, he gave Leon a disparaging look.

"It was the only place outside home that you spoke positively about, Pietro . . ." Leon walked closer; his plans about what to say seeming useless now, so he gestured towards the building. "How about showing me around in there?"

Pietro shrugged. "Okay." He retraced his steps.

Leon followed. The ruin was just a shell of a place – no roof, its walls smothered in ivy. They walked into its only room. Piles of rank-smelling rubbish had collected where the fireplace would have been.

"Did you manage any sleep in here, Pietro?"

He shook his head. "Cold and windy. Rabbits scratching around, owls hooting." He smiled weakly. "So, I was not lonely . . ."

"That's something, then. Good. But weren't you scared? I would have been . . ."

"I was a bit scared. I had to be here, to do some thinking."

"A good place for it. I probably should do some too."

They went outside and sat down beside a boulder. The boy looked edgy, and drawn.

"Have you eaten?"

Pietro shook his head.

Leon opened his backpack, pulling out cans of soft drink,

packets of crisps and nuts, and some plums. He offered the food to him. "So did the thinking help?"

Pietro grabbed a can, drank greedily from it, then looked across at him. "It was about a lot of things . . ."

"Including me, the way I upset you with that letter?"

"No, it wasn't that . . ."

"So, what was it?"

Pietro's shoulders shuddered as the words began to spill out. How his father and Nonna had said not to mention his mother's name after she died, how the past was best forgotten. And how there was no-one else to talk to about her, no-one who knew her after they moved to another house. Only his mother's brother, but his father had fallen out with him. How his world was a lonely and unhappy place until he started helping out at the hotel. Looking after the trees, playing with the residents' children, until the drowning happened. Hating to talk to his counsellor every few days, but pretending it was all going well, for fear of upsetting Greta.

Leon did no direct questioning, allowing Pietro's words to wander anywhere. It took a good while for him to struggle through everything, stopping and starting, shaking and crying. Sometimes he gave up, his sobbing too persistent, especially when speaking of the bullying. At other times, a fiery resentment took over, Leon offering an arm round his shoulders to try and calm him, the boy wriggling away. Leon listened attentively, picking up on this and that, occasionally asking for clarification, piecing together an understanding of the boy's distress and concerns.

And as Pietro talked on, he managed to find a route out for

himself, making sense of things in his own way, sifting out what mattered most. Leon felt a tenderness towards him, that same fierce protectiveness he'd felt for Maria. His gut tightened as he thought of Greta. Was this him parenting the boy? So what? Because right now that was what he was needing.

"It helps to talk to you."

"Does it?"

"I have decided something."

"What's that?"

"That my art work must be my future. Father believes I cannot build a life from it, and that you are wrong to encourage me, but I can, I know I can."

"It's true your father and Nonna are unhappy about me – they think I upset you and caused you to run off. But your father knows you better than I do, he's always been there for you. You have to give him his place."

"You stick up for him? When I disappoint him – always? I try to please him. But it does not make a difference."

Umbrage crowded Pietro's face, and Leon regretted his comments. But Leon could see he was settling down a bit, his voice steadier, his words more measured. He pushed more food in front of him.

"Leon – it was you who helped me see I have choices, you who said I had to think for myself." He shrugged. "I believe all of that. But I also believe in fate, like the Greek poets did – Homer, and Hesiod. You will think that makes me all mixed up, but Greta believes in fate too. She told me about an American writer she liked reading."

"Who was that?"

"Martha Nussbaum. She wrote about how you need to trust in uncertain things, in things that seem beyond your control. What I trust is that whatever is put in my way, I will do my art, I'll insist to Father. This is my fate – it is what I am fated to do."

Leon liked the boy's verve. "So, this is where your thinking's taken you?"

He nodded. "But Father will not be happy." His eyes grew large and intense. "And you, Leon, those poets would say it was fate that brought you out here, they would say your daughter sent you. We both needed fate's help, did we not? I found my art work. You got your chance to rescue your life. It is my belief that your life back home was a kind of drowning."

Pietro's words alarmed Leon, reminding him of the boy Danny in *The Shining*, with his gift of second sight. "Well . . ."

"Your money-making magic wasn't helping, was it? You needed to conjure up something different, so fate brought you out here."

"I'm not so sure about that . . ."

"But you discovered new things out here, didn't you? New things to bring into your life and believe in."

"Did I?"

"I am sure of it. And the hermit – your monk Benghi – the man who passed his whispering gift to me. He is here with us, Leon, I see him lurking. He was there when the boy was drowning, just for a moment." He flapped his arms around, excited but exasperated. "You must have seen what I see. Those times when the world is still, when nature comes to you. You must have felt the trees trembling, smelt that scent in the air. The plants, the stars, the olive trees, all listening, all talking . . ."

Leon thought of Danny again, and the hold the hotel had on him. But another world was building and tugging: his plans for his life back home, and his urge to see Kay.

"I accept that you see and feel these things. Whatever you find can help you – you should enjoy, accept and celebrate it – not let it become a barrier between you and real life."

Pietro looked indignant. "But all that is part of me. It is me, it's what makes sense to me, it's what makes sense of me."

Leon nodded. "I know. But right now, we have things to deal with. You've been skipping school, and I don't blame you. But you want to get back to return to your art, so we need to make school safe for you. Can you talk to your father about it?"

"Father? Huh. He would think I am stalling, being soft and spineless."

"Is there anyone else?"

"My uncle maybe, he is my mother's sister. But Father fell out with him, he does not like me to see him."

"Then, at your school? You need to work out which teachers, which students could be on your side, be there to help you."

Pietro seemed on the verge of sobbing again. "I don't know how to work that out . . ."

Leon was frantic with pity for him. "Let me think . . ."

Pietro interrupted. "Greta could help me, but she is sick. Is she going to die? Or get sick and not have a proper life?" His voice was wobbling. "She will die, won't she? And you, Leon – you will be gone."

Leon swiftly explained that Greta had hopes for more active years, and he had a plan about how to help her, during that time.

"Is it a good plan?"

"It is. And I'll tell you something – what you were saying about fate makes some sense to me. Because if I hadn't come here, and met you and Greta, I wouldn't have tackled my drinking. That means I can try and work things out now, back home with my girlfriend. Do you see?"

Pietro nodded.

"We can speak to Greta. Shall we phone her from the village? She could let your father know you're here, and are going back home. She might even come and fetch you."

Pietro nodded, looking relieved.

"I believe she would help your father understand what's happened. She could talk to the teachers as well."

"Promise me your plan to help her will happen."

"I will do my best."

Pietro stood up and looked around him. "I can sense something powerful, can't you?"

Leon hesitated. "Sense what?"

"Our plans. Can't you feel something stirring in the soil of our past, in our village's history, pushing us forward? We've being promised more than we know, we must now learn how to be ready for our future in seeking out ways to nourish it."

Leon smiled, leading the boy towards the village. He thought about something his own grandmother used to say: You can't put old heads on young shoulders. Hadn't this boy proved her wrong?

Southern Italy – July 1998

LEON turns left to drive slowly along the dirt road. The olive grove looks different, tellingly vibrant, he supposes because it's better cared for. The road opens up to a view of his hotel building, and something seems to vibrate. A greeting . . . or a warning?

Kay leans towards him, grinning. "Wow! This is the place – exciting! I can't wait to explore."

He parks the car, reflecting on how his life has changed since last he was here, and how Kay has helped with that. A saying comes into his head – Change is the end result of all true learning. He believes that's true. It was written by an educationalist he recently came across, Leo Buscaglia: an Italian immigrant living in Los Angeles, originally from Aosta in Northern Italy.

They clamber out of the car, and stare around.

"Is this the way it used to be? Or has it changed?"

"It feels different from the old hotel. Something more peaceful about it, yet more welcoming. Come on, let's take a look around, we've plenty of time."

He leads her over to the viewing platform where they take in the ocean, and shows her the path he used to walk down to the Port. Then he turns to point out the hillside where his family's village lies, speaking of the things that kindled his interest in history.

"It's a shame, Kay, that you can't meet Greta. She was the one who started me on that journey."

"I know." She pauses. "And I've never asked, but often wondered . . . did you have a relationship with her?"

"With Greta, out here?"

"Yes."

"You mean a sexual one?"

She nods.

"No way."

"So, was there no chemistry at all?"

He laughs, shaking his head. "Oh Kay, you're such a pest, poking around in my psyche. All that matters is that I'm with you. I'm so lucky."

Just as she is about to reply, he steals her words from her with a kiss, but knows this won't put an end to them.

Greta's funeral has taken place some days ago – for family only. Today's service is a memorial celebration, in the open air, in the central cloister area. A woman called Matilde is leading it. Leon has noticed Pietro, sitting near the front with a slim and elegantly dressed young woman who is nursing a baby. She must be his wife. He's reminded of being with Sue at his mother's funeral, sitting in a pew with their baby Maria.

Matilde speaks fervently in Italian: "*Sarò sempre grato per l'opportunità unica che Greta mi ha dato di gestire, per suo conto, questo centro che abbiamo qui . . .*"

". . . I will always be grateful for the once in a lifetime opportunity Greta gave me to run this magnificent centre, on her behalf . . ." She goes on to give thanks to the anonymous benefactor whose trust fund enabled Greta to buy the hotel and develop it into a trauma centre, reverting back to its previous role of retreat. But as she begins showcasing the

99

centre's achievements, they are interrupted by Raphael, his stick clacking noisily on the marble tiles. His gait is skewed, following a stroke, which Pietro had written to Leon about. The funds Leon sent to help with his recovery were disdainfully returned.

Matilde outlines the kinds of traumas they work with, and what treatments are offered. She says that initially the work they did was controversial, but Greta was pivotal in motivating everyone to carry on. She offers up praise for their resident artist and art therapist – Pietro.

Next she talks next about Greta's qualities – her resilience, her determination, her capacity to live with her own pain while healing other people's. Her small ego, her ability to help people face their own fears, pain and vulnerability; her drive to learn from other people, her openness to ideas that challenged her own. And how she aimed to create a melting plot of rich and fervent debate, fostering constructive scrutiny of everything they were trying to achieve.

Leon sees that he never fully knew or appreciated Greta. Finding him on the brink of tears, Kay gently wraps her fingers round his, as Mathilde steps aside for Greta's mother.

The woman appears strained and weary; she looks around those present as if searching for a knowing face. Her voice is hesitant as she begins by explaining she has recently buried her husband, and will therefore speak only briefly. She talks about his love for their daughter, and her love for him. About how a daughter should not precede a mother in death. Eventually breaking down, she finishes by saying how Greta made light of problems, how kind she was to both good and bad, and sought out the neediest.

Footsteps signal someone walking towards the front, a man pauses there to put an arm round Greta's mother's shoulder, whispering a few words before helping her back to her seat. He returns and introduces himself as Greta's brother, pulling some notes from his pocket.

"*Benvenuti a tutti – Greta, la mia sorella maggiore . . .*" "Hello everyone – how we all loved my older sister Greta. How can such a splendid person be snatched so cruelly from us? We cannot believe it. But yet, of course, we can and must. Because the pain burns deep and constant, we have to stare it in the face, learn to accept it. We have to love and help one another to live with the anguish of such a death, seek comfort and support in the caring hands of each other."

Leon hadn't known she had a brother; he thinks he looks nothing like her. But as he watches and listens, he recognises shared traits: the cautious choice of words, the warm but direct way of talking, the unrushed pace of delivery. The man finishes by saying that Greta could never bare malice, and that she even forgave her cancer. "She was right, was she not? For there is sweetness in forgiveness; resentment tastes bitter."

He asks others to come forward and speak, even if with just a few sentences. A few do so. Finally, Pietro stands, carefully handing the baby to his wife, and walking solemnly to the front.

"*Benvenuti a tutti.* The seeds of my involvement in this place were sown by Greta. Connecting with her helped to validate my hunch that the building and its grounds

needed to reconnect with their past, with previous service to the community, and with their intimate union with
nature – especially with the olive trees. This truth whispered
to me, the truth of this place. I knew the land had been a
spiritual place, a place of healing, of freeing people to find
their own path. We worked to sustain its destiny as a place
where the natural environment would be hallowed, nour-
ished and respected."

He pauses, scanning his audience, his eyes fleetingly falling on Leon. Leon imagines Greta would have thought very
carefully about how best to involve Pietro, ensuring a fruitful
place for him in the Centre. At least, he thinks, he has helped
in that. As he listens to him, he is struck by his engaging presence and strong commitment. But a thought creeps up on
him: was his motive for helping Pietro and Greta simply a
sham?

"Everyone here loved Greta. She was unique. She had a way
of making you feel it was your contribution that was special,
you were the one going that extra mile. A gifted teacher, she
understood the process and value of learning. She harnessed
all you could give, made sure your skills and ideas prospered,
found ways to anchor them into the Centre. She helped us
learn from the master thinkers, those creative minds in the
fields of husbandry, philosophy, education, counselling and
trauma management.

"For me, she fostered my love of art, helped me believe
in and understand its therapeutic qualities. Nature and art
became twin kindnesses here, key vehicles for recovery. Long
before I began my training, I had a period of hurting – a

double bereavement – but Greta never gave up on me. And when my Nonna died last year, she was there for me again, in spite of her pain from late-stage cancer."

He invites everyone to stand and join in applauding Greta's work and her life. After this, Mathilde returns to close the service, inviting people to meet her outside for a tour of the Centre. A spate of anxiety takes hold of Leon.

Out in the sunshine, Mathilde beckons Pietro to stand by her side as she outlines the process for touring the Centre, explaining some residents are victims of torture and genocide. As he listens, Leon spots Raphael walking across to his car, realising he has not yet spoken with him. They then re-enter the building, named to the right of the entrance as the Luca Centre. Mathilde guides them to a plaque in the lobby:

QUESTO CENTRO TRAUMATOLOGICO PRENDE IL NOME

LUCA MACRINA,

CHE QUI PERSE TRAGICAMENTE LA VITA ALL'ETÀ DI TRE ANNI.

È DEDICATO ALLE MANI GUARITRICI DELLA CREATIVITÀ,

GENTILEZZA E IL NOSTRO MONDO NATURALE.

SI FONDA SULLE IDEE AUDACI E CORAGGIOSE DI

GRETA GESSANI,

E RESO POSSIBILE DA

UN BENEFATTORE ANONIMO.

THIS TRAUMA CENTRE IS NAMED AFTER

LUCA MACRINA,

WHO TRAGICALLY LOST HIS LIFE HERE AT THE AGE OF THREE.

IT IS DEDICATED TO THE HEALING HANDS OF CREATIVITY,

KINDNESS, AND OUR NATURAL WORLD.

IT IS FOUNDED ON THE BOLD AND BRAVE IDEAS OF

GRETA GESSANI,

AND MADE POSSIBLE BY

AN ANONYMOUS BENEFACTOR.

She then goes on to explain how part of the funding is reserved and invested for future innovative, evidence-based approaches, especially art-based ones. She turns to Pietro. "Tell us how, Pietro."

He smiles, beginning by saying he believes in something Herbert Marcuse once said, about how art breaks open a dimension inaccessible to other kinds of experience. A dimension in which human beings and nature no longer stand under the same old laws of established reality. He then explains how art therapy works – as a means of emotional and creative release, the relaxation of mind and body, distraction from painful memories, building discipline and focus. "The whole process of making art," he tells them, "gives people the confidence to express and shape what lies within them into something communicable."

"He is an inspiration here," adds Mathilde, once he's finished. "He's also led on the therapies of the natural world. Once we've explored the Centre, he'll take you outside and into the grounds and garden, explaining our ethos and methods."

As Leon follows the group, he thinks how the Centre could have helped Sue – with her grief and trauma, the physical disfigurement, the agoraphobia, the asthma and her loss of will to live. He thinks of his own inadequacy in not being able to reach her. How she couldn't and wouldn't be helped by him – the person who'd caused her trauma.

Now he's here at last, he feels like a bystander – listening, watching, registering things, but wary of something. Just now, strolling through his old hotel, something almost overwhelmed him. But what? He feels less sure of himself, and who he was then, here, before. Was he broken? A drinker, whose wife couldn't stand him. A man suspicious of kindness. Kay had helped him, edged him towards his history degree, his masters in adult learning, research into learning routes for youngsters leaving care. He is content with his work as lecturer at the institute he founded, proud of the alternative models of practice he has been developing.

The group strolls on through the public areas, Mathilde explaining the different kinds of support, showing examples of residents' rooms and areas where workshops take place. Kay draws Leon's attention to residents' art work on the walls, some capturing specific features of the Centre: its topiary, the refurbished lily pond, the old gardeners' shed since upgraded into a gazebo. He finds some paintings signed by Pietro, works he imagines could sell for eye-watering sums. But why, he asks himself, is he measuring something's worth in money?

Mathilde taps on a door off the central corridor, and a woman of slight build emerges. "Simona, *ciao*. Thank you for offering your time to tell us about your experience as a resident at the Centre."

Simona smiles at everyone, showing no signs of nervousness. "*Benvenuti a tutti*." She points at a painting on the wall, depicting a turbulent skyscape. "This is my painting, the beginnings of my recovery. Before I had help for my trauma here, I would not have thought to lift a brush. But painting this picture outdoors, on the cliff side, with the smell of the sea, the sight of the surf, the sound of the sea birds – it set me on a journey. Of course, it was a faltering one, with plenty stops and starts, but helped me believe in living again."

Leon wonders – how many times has she offered up this story? A fund-raising tool, maybe? But he cautions this voice in his head.

Mathilde thanks Simona, and hands over to Pietro, who leads them outside to explore the grounds.

Pietro walks the group at a leisurely pace, identifying the functions of the different areas, pointing out features developed by the residents, explaining the life cycles of some of the plants. He goes on to speak about the work of Doctor Matthew in developing the Minerva Gardens, and how they inspired his work in the grounds here with residents.

"As residents work the land, they learn how it sustains them, both psychologically and physically; they then come to respect it and nurture it in return. That transmutes into respect for themselves, and mutual nurturing and respect for each other. Everything is interconnected."

After some questions, the group begins to disperse, and Greta's mother approaches. She speaks in halting English.

"Signore Leon, I know of you from Greta. You lost a daughter, tragically, I am sad for you, I hope that you have found some ways of comfort. We both share in this grief, yes?

But I say to you, that we all take comfort in Greta having her dreams fulfilled." She lays a hand on Pietro's shoulder. "And you too helped this man, did you not? You believed in his ambition, his passion for his art."

"Thank you for your kind words, Signora Gessani. I did indeed believe in Pietro. And in your Greta too, and everything she had to offer. Signora, please accept my condolences for your loss of a remarkable daughter."

"Thank you, Signore Leon. And because of this, how do I say, this connection we have . . . in the morning, will you return to be with me and Pietro, to say our final goodbyes to Greta?"

Leon nods and smiles, unsure what this is to involve.

"Until tomorrow."

Pietro summons them over to a table shaded from the sun. He asks about Leon's time in the UK, expressing approval for his 'new vocation of teaching'. Leon smiles, thinking about their last time together, up on the hillside. Kay asks Pietro about his training.

"I was very lucky to win a scholarship funded through a school trust fund, to do an access course to gain entry to a prestigious art academy in Milan. That scholarship was the beginning of Father's change of mind, and wanting to have me back in his life again."

"You don't mean he disowned you?" asks Kay.

Pietro shrugs. "I was just a mixed-up kid then, you know – in a mess after witnessing Luca's death. I needed the distraction. But for Father, it was a bad distraction, and a damaging one, and he blamed Leon for it."

"Yes, Leon did tell me about that." She glances across at him.

Pietro smiles. "Your man taught me the yin and yang, how to take the rough with the smooth." He smiles at Leon. "I should tell you what happened, you know, after you left me that day . . ."

"Yes, go ahead," Kay says, pushing her chair back from the table. "But let me give you some space to talk together. I can see your wife over there with the baby, Pietro, I'll go and join them."

"Thank you." He waves to his wife, then turns to Leon. "You know, it wasn't the best of times, returning to Father and Nonna after hiding away like that."

"I imagine it wasn't."

"And yet in a way, it was good; because it made for some change. I stuck up for you, and they didn't like that. They wanted – you know – to make you a scapegoat. Father blamed Greta too, for introducing you to me. Then, the next day, a man turned up at the house, someone running an apprentice-ship scheme. They wanted my name on the waiting list that day. At such a young age! I'm sure it was a good scheme – for the right person."

"They thought it was right for you, I suppose."

"I refused to do as they said. So, they sent me to live with my uncle until I changed my mind. Then Uncle Lorenzo and Greta spoke together, and helped sort out the bullying prob-lems at school."

"And you stayed on with your uncle?"

"Yes, he is a good man. I stayed until I went to Milan."

"Did you make it up with your father?"

"You could say that."

"And what about Nonna, Pietro? She wasn't well, was she?"

"It was a heart attack. She didn't recover, she died seven months later. I wondered if it was all my fault, for causing her worry, but Greta stopped me thinking that. In spite of her illness, she found the space to help me."

"I'm glad, but I'm sorry about Nonna. And how is your father's health? I would have liked to have spoken with him, because things were never settled between us."

"He copes well after the stroke. He is head chef now – for the Centre." He laughs. "So, you see, he found a way to keep an eye on me . . ."

"Ah . . ."

"But he wants to see you. Perhaps you have booked a meal out somewhere, but he insists on bringing dinner to you tonight, in your chalet. He would also like to eat with you, and to talk, if you could be happy with that?"

Leon thinks about this. "That's kind. But I'll need to ask Kay . . ." He turns to look for her, but she is right behind him with the baby, juggling her around and making funny faces.

When Leon returns to the chalet, he finds Kay fast asleep on the bed. He leaves her sleeping until it's almost time for Raphael to arrive.

"You should have woken me earlier, and we could have had a chat. And does our chef really have to eat with us?"

"I know, it would be nice just to eat on our own. But he'd be hurt if we refused him, and I doubt he'll linger."

Leon prepares the dinner table while Kay washes and changes. He's finding it strange being back with people he hasn't seen for years. But that must be the case with memorial services, he thinks. At least Greta's had been small and intimate, possibly at her request.

When Raphael arrives, Kay is still in the bathroom. He is trailed by two young kitchen hands, carrying stainless steel canisters which they ask to be kept hot in the chalet kitchen. Raphael props a package of something to the side of the door.

"*Bueno*, Raphael. This is so good of you," Leon offers in Italian.

Raphael nods. "It is a chance to talk properly. It has been a long time, and things went unsaid. But I will speak English, for the sake of your friend Kay. But perhaps she is your girlfriend, yes?"

Leon nods. Kay joins them, her hair damp from the shower, thanking Raphael for the food. As Raphael accepts a drink of cold beer from the fridge, there is a knock at the door – their cold starters. They take their drinks, Leon with sparkling water, over to the table. They begin by discussing the memorial service, and how Greta had hoped to see other Centres established. About Greta's mother and how she is coping, about future developments at the Centre. Raphael interjects with a few sour notes: about teething troubles back at the start, personality conflicts amongst staff, some residents 'taking the Centre for granted'. Leon listens with an open mind, conceding there's a downside to everything, but thinking this verges on gossip.

"There has been speculation about the anonymous benefactor," he adds.

"Really?"

"Yes. Naturally, we all are curious about him."

"It could be a woman, though?" asks Kay.

Raphael nods. "But we assume it is someone who knows Greta. For after all, it was insisted that she be the one to be allowed to lead the work." In a querying way, he glances at Leon.

So, thinks Leon, he suspects me.

"And also, around the time that this money was given, a legacy was gifted to the school, from which my son benefited. Again, it was anonymous. Was that this same rich man too? Hmm. Where there is an emptiness of information, chatter will arrive and fill the void."

"I suppose people give anonymously for various reasons," Kay offers, looking uncomfortable. "Modesty? Privacy? Wanting to remain neutral over how it is spent?"

"Or," Raphael continues, "because they do not want to be inviting some trouble. Perhaps they want to arrange, in advance, for some, more than others, to benefit, without the criticism for that arriving at their door. Remember that other benefactor? That man who rebuilt this place we have here, after the fire? The very rich son of a slave trader? His bequest – it was guilt money. Yes? So, you see?" He looks at Leon again. "So, there is clean money, is there not? And there is guilt and dirty money."

Leon takes this as a dig, but holds back. He feels a modicum of fondness for the man, as in the end he didn't step in the way of his son's ambition. But he does judge him for tunnel vision. "It's great," he says, "to see all the good work Pietro is doing at the Centre. And his own painting has developed so well. I know you weren't so happy with him pursuing that – in the days when I was here before, and getting to know him."

"I doubted he had sufficient talent for it – to be an artist working on his own, making enough money for himself, and to support a family. His mind might have been fixed on that, but I am glad I persuaded him not to do it."

"You did? I'm not sure what you mean, Raphael . . ."

"Me and Greta. We both did it together, we persuaded him to take a job at the Centre instead."

"Oh." Leon feels confused. "I thought he'd made his own path, there. But I know that you felt I'd interfered – come between father and son – all of that."

"Well – yes, Leon – you did interfere." He looks away, and towards Kay. "He will have spoken to you about this? How he went away back to the UK – that time when my boy got lost – without even seeking me out to explain?"

"I think this is just between you and Leon, Raphael."

But the tone of Raphael's voice has become clipped, his expression stern, his back tightly straightened. Leon is reminded of Sue's demeanour as she criticised him about his trips away – as being too long and frequent. Her hurt expression when Maria came to his defence. He should have spoken to Maria about that.

"You see, Kay, on one day Pietro became lost, he did not return home to us – but not lost from Signore Leon, it seems. My boy was disappeared up in the hills out there beyond the village . . ." He gestures at the window. "But Leon was there, with him, and I did not receive an explanation."

"That's true, Raphael, and I want to apologise."

"Kay – we were badly worried. Leon went up there after him – but he did not let us know. Pietro made a phone call from the village – not to me, but to Greta. Why did Leon not insist for Pietro to ring me? Twelve years go passed, but no apology. Then your Leon comes back when Greta's ashes are still warm, dares to stare me in the eye, just as if nothing was happened." He stops to glance at Kay again; she glances back, but icily. "Ah. Perhaps, then, I have gone too far? Kay – sorry. I did not intend to upset you . . ."

"It's okay, Raphael," she says. "And your food is delicious, don't allow yours to go cold. Look, it's always good to clear the air. But let's have a breather for a moment, get that hot food out of the oven. We can talk this thing out then." She throws Leon a look which signals caution.

The main course is a colourful sea food risotto. Partly prepared in advance, Raphael has finished it with ingredients chilled separately in the kitchen.

"It must," says Kay to Raphael, as they settle into eating, "have been a great loss when your wife died. And Pietro being so young."

"It was, Kay. And things, they became harder still – with that tragic drowning. Then you coming here, Leon – getting involved . . . all very good at the start. But it made me feel worthless, less of a father to him, it made me feel I never helped him with – as it is called – his trauma. There you were with your money, buying him things, giving him strange ideas. Instead of doing what you had come here for – to properly discover your family history." His voice becomes slightly menacing. "You market gardeners. Exploiting all our small businesses, taking them over, spoiling so many livelihoods, poisoning our soil with plastics and pesticides . . . you must go to ask Pietro about it . . ."

Leon's shoulders stiffen. "I was never told anything about that."

"Huh. Those fancy guides you took on, they charged a fancy price too, yes? They would not spin you a negative story, do themselves out of a decent tip . . ." He shook his head. "But to return to what I am saying. Your involvement, and your closeness to my boy. So much so that you go behind my back to give him a copy of the inquest report. Taking him into the past to all that, stirring up memories, what right had you? Encouraging his deceit in that, too. I would not have known had I not found it hidden at the bottom of a drawer, when I was sorting out his room after he left."

"Raphael – I can see how that would feel like a betrayal, would make you angry. Perhaps it was bad judgment on my part. If so, I am sorry."

"Perhaps? If so? Pah! It was Greta who helped me with my anger at it, it was she who taught me how to see it. Before you came, I was frightened of things going wrong, I was trying to work out how to do the things for him the way my wife might have done, but often failing. Then it started to get better – me, Pietro and my mother, we were living better with our grief. Pietro was working happy after school at the hotel. Then that tragic thing happened – the boy in the pond."

"I am so sorry for that. So, what did Greta teach you?"

"She explained how you were using him as a way to help

yourself. You used him to bring your own colour back into your life, to find a cheap way to forget your own grief." Raphael pauses, searching for some reaction in Leon.

Leon wonders – did Greta really say that? Or is this Raphael's take on it? He's not sure how to read the man. Is he being vindictive, or simply needing to speak the truth? Some things about him have his respect. Other things remind him of himself – his cynicism, skepticism, distrust of people. A man unable to deal with his own pain, seeking ways to blame other people for it. He feels tired and uneasy.

"A bad thing happened to you also, Leon, did it not?"

"It did. My daughter was murdered, as Greta told you."

"I am sorry for that. Such a thing never leaves you."

"That's true. A constant companion."

"It was a veil through which you saw the world, my son a useful distraction. But you should not give something conditionally. In return for your help, you demanded friendship and involvement in his life. That was wrong."

Kay speaks sharply to him: "For goodness's sake, Raphael, Leon only meant well, you're being very hard on him."

"It's alright Kay," says Leon, "I have to understand this. Raphael – I'm glad you're being honest with me, it's long overdue. I've thought about things while I was away, about things left unsaid, how I might have done things better by you. I thought about your grief, the loss of your wife, your mother's sadness losing a daughter, the grief always there in the room, unspoken of."

"It was, it was always there." Raphael is still eating his risotto, pushing his food onto his fork, then releasing it, like a cat playing with a mouse. He sits silently over it for a while before getting up from the table with his plate: "I thank you for your apology, Leon. Now I shall fetch our lemon tart from the fridge. It is of my very own making."

Kay looked at Leon as Raphael left the room. "That was heavy. Are you okay?"

Yes – but it was pretty gruelling. Still – good to clear the air."

"He's far more outspoken than you, eh? Gets quickly to the point. You like to trek around a bit, don't you? A detour here, some use of camouflage there . . ."

"You think so?"

Raphael returns with his tart. He has placed it on a local potter's dish, its rim festooned with hand painted leaves and lemons, its handles crafted like branches. He has divided the tart into portions.

"Please serve yourselves."

"This looks delicious," enthuses Kay, before forking a piece into her mouth.

"It is a local traditional recipe. But for me, to make it perfect, I need corn flour – for the filling – and iced water for the dough."

"We must be in one of the best regions for lemons," says Leon. "There's something about the area here that went back home with me, and still lives with me. The air, the sounds, the landscape. It all gets into your head, your bones, your very being. I like the Italians, I've missed them. Take you Raphael, we've had our differences, but you are of very strong character, and I respect your candour."

Raphael smiles. "You believe so? Greta told me that your stay here had brought the Italian out of you. And there is one thing that an Italian would never dream of doing, Leon . . ."

"And what is that?"

"To betray a friend. And Greta said that she believed that in you. In your loyalty. She saw it in the friendship you gave to my Pietro."

"That is true of Leon," says Kay. "You and Greta must be good judges of character."

But Leon feels raw, disturbed by the conversation, especially having Maria brought into it. The memorial service has pushed something out of place, and now he's thinking of her cat again, its neck hanging loose, blood seeping from its fur . . . he's hearing the doorbell, Maria saying I'll get that . . . her screams, him rushing to her, the sweat of fear on his neck, her distorted expression . . . Sue saying – *We have an enemy, then? No, he insists*, while all the time knowing what and who this is. Punishment for ignoring G's letters.

Leon tastes the pie, too sweet for his liking. "You must be so proud of your son, Raphael, he spoke so eloquently. And all his wonderful work at the Centre, he's found a niche there. His art work, yes, but also his healing – and his work in the natural world. That breadth of work could be more rewarding than simply working alone as an artist – away from the world, festooned in a studio."

"I am glad you recognise that. When he came home that time he was lost, I saw the first signs of the man he would be. I saw it in the way he stuck up for you, no matter what I said to him. It angered me, but I could not but respect him for it."

He gets up from the table, reaches for the package propped against the wall. "Here – this is for you, from Pietro. He has a soft spot for you still, you see."

Leon takes it, and walks over to the table to unwrap it. Raphael pulls a letter from his pocket, placing it on the table. "He gave this for you too."

The package contains a picture – a collage, each cut of a different texture. Leon looks down at it, thinking there's something Picassoesque about it, although its compelling unity is typical of Pietro's work.

Raphael examines it with him. "He said to tell you it's in the tradition of Cubism."

Leon's never much liked that school, but this piece is stunning and unsettling. The cut-outs contain hints of a snow plough, topiary work, ivy climbing up a building, a girl with curls like Maria's, rowing a boat. And there is a pond sheened with algae, with a fountain shaped like a boy riding a fish. He can't remember telling Pietro about the snow plough, or about rescuing Maria from a rowing boat. But he must have.

He stares down at the letter and decides to read it later.

After Raphael leaves, a young man and woman arrive from the kitchens to take the remains of the meal away.

"That was more than a mild confrontation," Kay says, once they have left.

"Yes, I suppose it was, I'm still taking it in. But Kay, I'm exhausted, I think that's more than enough for today. Let's sit quietly for a while, maybe take a second look at the painting?"

Kay suggests a walk in the grounds instead, but once out

there, the air is humid and they're pestered by mosquitos. Leon is not in need of conversation, and keen to go back inside. After wandering in very near silence for a while, they decide to do just that.

He follows her into the bedroom. It's only just gone ten o'clock, but she starts to undress. All he wants to do is sleep, so he's hoping she isn't wanting sex.

"You know Leon, you're very modest, not wanting people to know you were the benefactor. Do you think Raphael has guessed?"

Leon shrugs. "Probably. And, clearly, you have too."

"It wasn't that difficult. But look – you've done some wonderful things out here. For Greta, for the area, and for Pietro. He's grown up into a grand young man."

"He has," Leon replies, wanting to get himself out of further conversation.

"The man was really having a go at you about stuff . . . ."

"He was hoping to unsettle me. He's still resentful, as you could see."

"Do you begrudge him for it? I suppose he was saying a few conciliatory things just before he left."

"Begrudge him for not trusting me with his son? I did at the time; but I understand him better now. I'm glad he's cleared the air."

"Good, I'm glad."

But Leon's not feeling glad, not really. Grateful to understand the man better, yes, but something has started to shift and become unstable.

"So, how did you work out I was the donor?"

"It just seemed the kind of thing you would want to do. It explains your continuing interest in things out here, and in wanting to come back."

"You know me better than I do, I think . . ."

Kay laughs and disappears into the bathroom; Leon starts to undress, ashamed he'd never recognised Raphael's vulnerability. But today has had its joys, any sadness tempered by seeing the fruits of Greta's work and witnessing Pietro's achievements. By the time he's washed and back in the bedroom, Kate is in bed. He clambers in, finding it far too warm between the sheets, but glad the day will soon be over.

Kay edges closer, rumpling his hair and kissing his forehead. "I know you don't really want to talk, but the way Raphael went on, you'd think he was trying to sabotage your good feelings about funding the centre."

Leon grunts with exhaustion. "Yeah, I think he was – when he was banging on about the other benefactor paying a penance for living off profits from slavery. I guess he was insinuating there might be a similar story behind me."

"But he must know there's no story, surely?"

"There's the story of the death of my daughter, and the damage it caused, and the one about how I got over-involved in Pietro's life. He seemed to be teasing out parallels."

She reaches for his hand. "The death of your daughter was a devastating tragedy. But not something you need to pay a penance for."

"Yeah." Something irks him. "Except I think he may have come across a grain of truth." He's surprised to hear himself say this, but it's like there's a slow burn licking around him, as unwelcome images rise up in his mind. G. The man thin and willowy, stubbly beard, red straggles of hair and pocks on his face. Hunched shoulders, a seedy fisherman's sweater, baggy mustard cords, an army stores rucksack. His name was Gerry.

She edges even closer. "You mustn't let yourself think that. And as for Raphael – don't let him unsettle you. Think of Pietro's painting. And the letter – have you opened it?"

"Not yet."

"Well, just think of the difference you've made to Pietro's life, how fulfilled he is by what he's doing. You can tell, can't you?"

The bed is clammy and hot, and so is her body. She's wrapping herself around him, reaching for him. Stroking his penis while whispering and purring, sounding a bit like that tree. He isn't liking it all that much – now Raphael's rant and his own shabby memories are getting bound up with his reluctant erection. It feels like some grubby illicit liaison, the rhythm slicing through his thoughts, disturbing his ways of holding his stories together.

"I'm sorry," he says, "but I can't keep this up." He laughs thinly. "Literally." Peeling back the covers, he stares glumly at his wilting penis, then starts to come down on her. She pulls away.

"It's alright, Leon. You're tired. I can sort myself out if I want to."

Leon slumps back down in the bed. For a while, they don't speak.

"There's something going on, Leon, isn't there?"

"Sorry?"

"Something lurking around between us . . ."

"What?"

"Something, or someone, isn't there?"

Leon once more thinks of *The Shining*, the young boy's sense of a presence taking over his life. He thinks of Raphael accusing him of trying to take over Pietro's life. He thinks of Gerry, and it's just as if that acrid smell of his fisherman's jumper is in the room with him.

"It's that man Gerry. Even out here, I can't stop thinking of him . . ."

"Maria's killer? I've never heard you use a name for him before."

He sighs.

"Leon, listen. He's dead and gone, he took his own life. A disturbed and damaged man, who was fixated. Fixated on you, your life, the life of the family...not worthy of the smallest of thoughts . . ."

"I can't stop asking myself things, though. And thinking how he must have had a family of his own."

"You don't need to know about any of that. Is this because you never got your time in court?"

"He came up on the stage you know, I never told you that. It wasn't a case of some sociopath watching from the audience and developing a fixation on me . . ."

"But he must have had some kind of psychiatric condition."

Cause and effect, cause and effect, he thinks to himself . . . whatever the science might say, we decide on our versions of events, depending on what comforts us most. He thinks of Sue's mother's words, over the phone, the day after the murder: *It should have been you who got killed, Leon, there would have been some natural justice in that. Who would want you in their life now, Leon, after all that has happened? You could have stopped it.*

"I'm done for Kay, I'm sorry. Let's get some sleep."

"Alright then, have it your way. I don't suppose adding one more to the list will hurt . . ."

"Oh. You mean one more wilted cock?"

"I'm meaning another of those half-finished conversations that are crowding out our relationship."

Leon grunts and turns away from her.

But he only manages two hours of sleep before waking and needing to empty his bladder. He's regularly dreaming about Sue again, since Kay resumed asking questions. As the flow trickles to an end, he remembers Pietro's letter, wanders through to the table in the sitting room, where he rips it open. It's written in Italian, beginning with an invitation to a ceremony the next morning to scatter Greta's ashes. Then the letter turns to other things:

As you wrote in your only letter to me, I say in mine: thank you for our friendship.

But Leon, I see that something troubles you, something wanting to be resolved. Just as you saw something troubling me, that time. So, allow me this, to reflect your own words back to you:

Life is full of contradictions, yin and yang.

It can be hard to listen to your inner voice.

Will we grow, or will we wither?

So, are you open to learning, Leon? As you asked me to be?

I believe in you and in your future.

In friendship

Pietro

| 2 |

Pietro arrives at ten thirty the following morning, cradling an urn encrusted with tiny shards of sea glass. It has been inscribed. As they walk across to the Centre, Leon thanks him for the painting, talking about the things he most liked about it, but not querying its meaning. Pietro accepts his complements with grace.

"Was it you who decorated the urn?" asked Kay.

"Yes. It was one last thing I could do for her, and it helped me start coming to terms with the loss."

Leon thinks how the last thing he did for Maria was to transfer money into her account. If only it had been words or gestures of love. And nothing he might have said or done could have made amends to Sue. He still sees her injuries, the bits of flesh. Her mouth slashed, an ear part-severed, blood pooling in an eye socket, pieces of finger scattered about.

Pietro leads them to the left façade of the building, where the dining room extension was. There the umbrella tree rises up in splendid freedom, its trunk licked by the sun, its canopy swaying in the breeze. The surrounding ground has been carefully tended, and beneath the tree Leon finds a garden laid out with hostas, already in bud.

He clutches Pietro's arm. "So here is your tree."

"You still like our Luna Tigre?" he asks, gingerly laying down the urn upon a table placed amongst the hostas.

"I do."

Leon hadn't noticed it yesterday; something held him back from seeking it out. Pietro beckons them to sit at a bench over to one side, explaining they are early, with time to chat.

"Greta designed the little garden below the tree. I love hostas – they represent devotion and friendship."

"It's beautiful," Leon says. "Don't you think so, Kay?"

"It is indeed. What species is the tree, Pietro?"

"A stone pine, known locally as an umbrella tree. Did Leon tell you I felt drawn to it from when I was a child?"

"He told me you had a tree."

"I took responsibility for it. It needed me to be its whisperer. And I had a need for the tree." He glances at Leon. "You were meant to be its whisperer too, you know. Like me, and your hermit ancestor. Something made me know that. I was its guardian, then I was ill, you came along, the tree tuned to you, tried to reach out to you."

"You'll never make a tree whisperer of me, Pietro, I'm still too much of a skeptic. I grant you though, you brought the world with which the tree connects into my inner world. I thank you for that."

Pietro looks back at Kay. "We whisperers are not weirdos, and there are many of us. We know that trees live long and wisely. They whisper; we whisper back. They tell us things about ourselves. They play their part in rituals, they serve as conduits of healing. They make us brave, they give us strength, but only if we ask, returning their kindness. The Japanese worship them, they share in the practice of forest bathing, their way of enabling their inner spirit to commune with nature."

"There's nothing weird about you, Pietro. But there is something magical in the way you express your ideas and beliefs. Your respect for nature is inspiring."

People are drifting towards them. A young woman is steering Greta's mother along the path, others come forward to embrace Pietro. He offers warm words of welcome before delivering a brief tribute to Greta, then draws their attention to the tree.

"Once Greta acquired the old hotel building, she wanted to liberate this tree. A dining room extension had been built around it, and its trunk was covered in plastic. It was a symbol of all the things we hated seeing happening in the natural world. When the tree was freed, it began to change. Its trunk developed a healthy sheen, it reached out to the other trees again. As I stopped hearing its grief, I began to learn how to live with my own."

An applause strikes up. Then, at Pietro's request, each person comes forward to reach into the urn, grasp some cinders, and scatter them like grain amongst the hostas. As Leon takes his turn, he whispers some thanks to the tree. It doesn't whisper back, but as he scatters his ashes amongst the hostas he knows what it is that he needs to tell Kay.

Kay has insisted on seeing the village. But today it is stiflingly hot with hardly a hint of breeze, and she's finding the trek up the hillside hard going. He's asked her to walk in front, so he can go at her pace and point things out to her – the names of flowers, sea birds and trees. He even spots a blue throated lizard. Each time she tires, he suggests they stop and sit on the bank, close their eyes, and just breathe and listen.

Arriving in the village, Leon is shocked by the bustle and the change. The original buildings remain, but are now meticulously maintained. Many open spaces are filled with tasteful new-build. The streets are improved, and although the cobbles are retained, Leon feels the essence of the place is lost.

"Gentrification," he says to Kay. "Of the tourism variety."

They stroll along the resurfaced track towards Pietro's ruin, but as it comes into view, he realises it is inhabited. People are sitting around a picnic table positioned at the building's side; eating, gesticulating and laughing. Walking a little closer, he finds the original structure is unrecognisable, having been extended, clad in timber, with additions of a first-floor balcony and French windows. Feeling somehow that the building has betrayed him, he explains the changes to Kay.

She threads an arm through his. "I'm glad you saw it before, and as it was built to be. At least it's being kept going, for this and future generations. And the villagers would have welcomed some extra work helping to tart it up, don't you think?"

"It was our place for talking and thinking," he says. "Me and Pietro. I'd hoped you and I could go there too, and do our own talking." He slumps down onto the bank at the side of the track. "But this will do."

"You want to talk just now? Are you sure?"

He nods.

"Well – okay . . ."

"Thanks."

She sinks down beside him, and he begins. About how Raphael had stumbled across a truth, that he'd tried to buy off his own conscience by funding the Centre.

Kay interrupts: "I don't understand, that doesn't make sense. What are you talking about?"

"It won't make sense until I tell you the truth about what happened. I've never seen the truth myself before, not fully. I've been a coward, hiding away from it."

"The truth about what? Look, this sounds heavy. I'm hungry, Leon, and uncomfortable. Can't we find somewhere better to talk, some proper place for you to tell me?"

He shrugs. Deflated, he stands and helps her up. They set off back to the village, where they find a quiet café-bar. The waiter brings fresh orange juice, a green salad and smoked fish.

Leon hurriedly begins – with G, the man Gerry. That he was someone he'd chosen that night as a subject for hypnosis. It was against his better judgment, because the number volunteering to come up on stage to be hypnotised was small. The theatre ventilation was poor, the atmosphere airless and oppressive, he was desperate to keep things moving. Most of the volunteers ahead of Gerry he'd had to reject – none were suggestible enough to be hypnotised. The very keen Gerry was suggestible, but Leon cautioned himself, seeing signs of emotional vulnerability. Such a person could flip, or be damaged; although the risk was slight. Leon asked some screening questions, checking for phobias etc. Nothing emerged, so he selected him.

"But didn't all ticket holders have to sign a disclaimer?"

He nods, telling her this is where everything went wrong. Several days after the show, the man requested to speak with him, claiming the hypnosis had harmed him. "I refused, and within months everything escalated. Lawyers, complicated defences, claims for damages, a pending court case. He wanted his day in court, but my career would have been in tatters.

"But money, of course, was no object. So, I bought him off. With an enormous, eye-watering sum, on condition he signed a secrecy agreement, an NDA, to keep it out of the media. I'd misjudged it though, because it simply fuelled an obsessional hatred of me. He was clever; he found out about my family and began the stalking, pursuing us diligently. When I was on tour, he targeted Sue and Maria – letters claiming I was unfaithful, disgusting doorstep deposits, suspicious looking parcels. I paid a hitman to threaten him, but still it went on. It was a compulsion, I suppose."

"Christ, Leon." She reaches round the table and takes his arm. "You look terrible. You seem out of breath . . ."

He's close to hyperventilating as caustic words of Sue's spew around in his head . . . *You did it Leon, it was you that caused it, our daughter's death. Your arrogance, thinking you could just get rid of him. The way you treated him, just like a piece of dirt, you fuelled his anger, didn't you? Thought you could handle it all, along with that unscrupulous lawyer, that ghastly child-hood mate of yours . . .*

"Have you ever known real hatred, Kay? That blistering loathing for someone, when you're hungry for their death?"

She shakes her head.

"The consequences might have been less if I'd asked for help. But to keep the media out of it, I told lies. I lied to myself, saying I could get away with things, believing I had a right to that. I lied to Sue by saying I had no idea who he was. I never told her about paying him off, nor that he'd come up on stage with me. I said he was just a crazy guy who'd taken a dislike to me. I lied at the inquest too, I told them that exact same story. He was dead by then, and no-one could give his side."

He stops for a moment, trying to get his breathing steady, unable to look at Sue. "Before that, I was thinking about bumping him off. But that's a lie too, because I planned to, and I almost did it. I'd found a middle man, we'd agreed a sum, a date, with someone lined up to take him out. But I got cold feet at the eleventh hour. I called everything off."

His voice is hoarse, he's shaking, and he's feeling disgusted with himself. He eyes Kay, hesitating. "It's all about Sue, really. I ruined her life."

"About Sue? But your own life's been badly damaged too . . ."

"Sue saw Maria being killed, she tried to stop it. She'll never recover from her injuries."

"But you found them both there, covered in each

other's blood, witnessed those savage injuries. That was a huge trauma."

"I betrayed Sue. I could have stopped it."

By the time they start making their way back down the track, a gloomy sky is threatening. They walk in silence, a couple of times disturbing a rabbit. Dark clouds threaten from across the bay, but far below they can just make out the Centre. Kay insists they stop for a while and sit on the bank. Once settled, she says she has things she must say to him.

Leon is expecting this, and is relieved it has come. He's become weary of everything here: the changed village, his conversation with Raphael, Pietro's intensity.

"You must despise me now?"

"No, but some of the things you did are troubling. You've paid a price for your secrecy, and withholding the truth from yourself."

"I never was one for analysing myself."

"Perhaps that's your loss? And what was that thing you told me, that Greta said to Pietro? A good human being needs openness, a capacity to trust in things beyond their control? You need to trust that you can't change what happened, allow it to settle, leave it be. All this is classic, isn't it? Victims blaming themselves for the abuse they suffer. They think they've brought it on themselves, they even think they deserve it."

"I'm not a victim, Kay. I hate that word . . ."

"Oh yes you are, you've been seriously traumatised. It must have helped Sue to have you to blame, don't you think? That's been her safety valve."

"It's never occurred to me."

"Look, Leon. We don't want her pain wedged between us, festering away, worming into our relationship, slowly killing it off. I won't stand for it."

He sits there, feeling something easing off, thinking about the way Pietro worded his letter, remembering Raphael saying he admired his sense of loyalty. The skies are so dark, they can barely make out Vesuvius. Fat, hot drops of rain are plopping around them.

"Come on," she says.

They haul themselves up and tumble down the remains of the track, hardly noticing the umbrella tree as they run past it and into the centre, to begin packing their suitcases.

About the author

Mary Wilson lives in Glasgow. Much of her short story writing and poetry is rooted in social realism, sometimes drawing on her work experience in social care and addiction. Her work is published in the Federation of Writers' (Scotland) anthologies, and has been performed at the Edinburgh Fringe.

Printed in Great Britain
by Amazon